MIDWIVES O[...]

Welcome to Melbourne Victoria Hospital—
and to the exceptional midwives
who make up the Melbourne Maternity Unit!

These midwives in a million work miracles
on a daily basis, delivering tiny bundles of joy
into the arms of their brand-new mums!

Amidst the drama and emotion of babies
arriving at all hours of the day and night, when
the shifts are over, somehow there's still time
for some sizzling out-of-hours romance…

Whilst these caring professionals might come
face-to-face with a whole lot of love in their
line of work, now it's their turn to find
a happy-ever-after of their own!

Midwives On-Call

*Midwives, mothers and babies—
lives changing for ever…!*

Dear Reader,

A number of years ago my mother and I visited Australia. It was a beautiful and amazing country and I fell in love with it. I often speak of my visit to this day. When I was asked to join a group of world-class authors in writing the *Midwives On-Call* continuity, which was to be set in Australia, I jumped at the chance.

Ryan and Phoebe's story is set in Melbourne—one of the many places I had the pleasure of visiting. While in the area, my mother and I drove to the coast. On our way we visited a farm with a café much as Ryan and Phoebe do. We also went to see the Little Penguins come home. It's one of the most memorable things I've ever done. Like my characters, I had a lesson on what even the smallest of animals will do to take care of their young.

I'd be remiss if I didn't thank Fiona Lowe, one of my sister authors, who helped me— along with making me laugh—to work out the differences between the way the Aussies and the Americans speak. She was also wonderful in answering my questions about the area around Melbourne.

I hope you enjoy reading Ryan and Phoebe's love story. I like to hear from my readers. You can reach me at SusanCarlisle.com

Susan

HIS
BEST FRIEND'S
BABY

BY
SUSAN CARLISLE

® and TM are trademarks owned and used by the trademark owner and/or its licensee. Trademarks marked with ® are registered with the United Kingdom Patent Office and/or the Office for Harmonisation in the Internal Market and in other countries.

First published in Great Britain 2015
by Mills & Boon, an imprint of Harlequin (UK) Limited,
Large Print edition 2015
Eton House, 18-24 Paradise Road,
Richmond, Surrey, TW9 1SR

Special thanks and acknowledgement are given to Susan Carlisle for her contribution to the Midwives On-Call series.

ISBN: 978-0-263-25517-1

Harlequin (UK) Limited's policy is to use papers that are natural, renewable and recyclable products and made from wood grown in sustainable forests. The logging and manufacturing processes conform to the legal environmental regulations of the country of origin.

Printed and bound in Great Britain
by CPI Antony Rowe, Chippenham, Wiltshire

Susan Carlisle's love affair with books began when she made a bad grade in maths in the sixth grade. Not allowed to watch TV until she'd brought the grade up, she filled her time with books and became a voracious romance reader. She still has 'keepers' on the shelf to prove it. Because she loved the genre so much she decided to try her hand at creating her own romantic worlds. She still loves a good happily-ever-after story.

When not writing Susan doubles as a high school substitute teacher, which she has been doing for sixteen years. Susan lives in Georgia with her husband of twenty-eight years and has four grown children. She loves castles, travelling, cross-stitching, hats, James Bond and hearing from her readers.

Books by Susan Carlisle

Mills & Boon Medical Romance

Heart of Mississippi

The Maverick Who Ruled Her Heart
The Doctor Who Made Her Love Again

The Doctor's Redemption
Snowbound with Dr Delectable
NYC Angels: The Wallflower's Secret
Hot-Shot Doc Comes to Town
The Nurse He Shouldn't Notice
Heart Surgeon, Hero...Husband?

Visit the Author Profile page at
millsandboon.co.uk for more titles.

Joseph.
Thanks for being a great tool.

MIDWIVES ON-CALL

Midwives, mothers and babies—
lives changing for ever...!

**Enter the magical world of the Melbourne Maternity Unit and
the exceptional midwives there, delivering tiny bundles of joy on a
daily basis. Now it's time to find a happy-ever-after of their own...**

Just One Night? by Carol Marinelli
Gorgeous Greek doctor Alessi Manos is determined
to charm the beautiful yet frosty Isla Delamere...
but can he melt this ice queen's heart?

Meant-To-Be Family by Marion Lennox
When Dr Oliver Evans's estranged wife, Emily, crashes back
into his life, old passions are reignited. But brilliant Dr Evans
is in for a surprise... Emily has two foster children!

Always the Midwife by Alison Roberts
Midwife Sophia Toulson and hard-working paramedic
Aiden Harrison share an explosive attraction...but will they
overcome their tragic pasts and take a chance on love?

Midwife's Baby Bump by Susanne Hampton
Hotshot surgeon Tristan Hamilton's passionate night
with pretty student midwife Flick has unexpected consequences!

Midwife...to Mum! by Sue MacKay
Free-spirited locum midwife Ally Parker
meets top GP and gorgeous single dad Flynn Reynolds.
Is she finally ready to settle down with a family of her own?

His Best Friend's Baby by Susan Carlisle
When beautiful redhead Phoebe Taylor turns up on ex-army medic
Ryan Matthews's doorstep there's only one thing keeping them apart:
she's his best friend's widow...and eight months pregnant!

Unlocking Her Surgeon's Heart by Fiona Lowe
Brooding city surgeon Noah Jackson
meets compassionate Outback midwife Lilia Cartwright.
Could Lilia be the key to Noah's locked-away heart?

Her Playboy's Secret by Tina Beckett
Renowned English obstetrician Darcie Green
might think playboy Lucas Elliot is nothing but trouble—
but is there more to this gorgeous doc than meets the eye?

Experience heartwarming emotion and pulse-racing drama in
Midwives On-Call
this sensational eight-book continuity
from Mills & Boon Medical Romance

These books are also available in eBook format
from millsandboon.co.uk

CHAPTER ONE

WHAT AM I doing here? Phoebe Taylor asked herself for the hundredth time, pulling her light coat closer. She could no longer get it to meet in the middle. Bowing her head against a gust of Melbourne, Australia, wind, she walked on. It would rain soon.

She looked at the name on the street sign. Morris Lane. This was the correct place. Phoebe didn't even have to check the paper in her hand that was shoved into her pocket. She had it memorized. She'd read it often during the past few weeks.

When had she turned into such a pathetic and needy person?

It had happened slowly, over the last eight months as her middle had expanded. She'd always heard that a baby changed you. She'd had no idea how true those words were until it had happened to her. She was even more fearful of the changes she faced in the weeks ahead. The fact she'd be handling them all on her own, had no one to rely on, frightened her.

She started down the cobblestone street lined with town houses. Joshua had written that if she needed anything she could contact Ryan Matthews. But who was she to him? An old army buddy's wife. People said those types of things all the time but few meant them. But she had no one else to turn to. There were teachers she worked with, but they all had their own lives, husbands and children. They didn't have time to hold her hand. There were plenty of acquaintances but none that she would call on. She'd take this chance because Joshua had said to. And this was Joshua's baby.

But would this guy Ryan help her? Be there for her during the delivery afterwards? Take Joshua's place at the birthing suite? *Yeah, right.* She didn't see any man agreeing to that job. Who took on someone else's widow and unborn child? She could never ask that of him. Would she want to? She didn't know this man outside of Joshua saying he was an upstanding mate.

When the walls of reality had started closing in on her and panic had arrived, she'd been unable to think of where to turn. Joshua's letter had called to her. Seemed to offer her salvation. Phoebe inhaled and released a breath. She'd come this far. She wouldn't turn back now. What was the worst Ryan Matthews could do? Send her away? Act like he'd never heard of her?

What she was sure of was she didn't want to feel alone anymore. She wanted someone to lean on. Be near a person who had a connection to Joshua. Hear a story or two that she could tell her son or daughter about their father. Joshua and Ryan had been brothers in arms. Been there for each other. Joshua had assured her in his last letter seven months ago that if she needed anything, *anything*, Ryan was the person to find. Desperate, she was going to his house to see if that was true.

Phoebe located the house number. It was painted above the door in black against the white frame of the Victorian house. The car traveling down the street drew her attention for a second. She pulled the paper out and looked at the address again, then at the entrance once more.

Studying the steps to the door, she hesitated. Now she was stalling.

What was she going to say to this guy?

She'd been rehearsing her speech for days and still didn't know if she could get it out. On the tram coming across town she'd practiced again but couldn't seem to get it right. Everything she'd planned made her sound crazy. Maybe she was. But she had to say something, give some explanation as to why she'd turned up on his doorstep.

Hi, I'm Phoebe Taylor. You were a friend of my husband's. He said if I ever needed anything to come see you. So here I am.

That should get his attention. She placed a hand on her protruding middle and chuckled dryly. *His first thought will probably be I'm here to accuse him of being the father.*

The wind gusted again as she mounted the steps. There were no potted plants lining them, like most of the other houses. Holding the handrail, she all but pulled her way up to the stoop. Could she get any bigger? Her midwife Sophia had assured her she could, and would.

After catching her breath, Phoebe knocked on

the door. She waited. Thankfully, the small alcove afforded her some shelter from the wind.

When there was no answer, she rapped again. Seconds went by and still no one came. She refused to go back home without speaking to Ryan. It had taken her months to muster the courage to come in the first place. It was getting late, surely he'd be home soon.

To the right side of the door was a small wooden bench. She'd just wait for a while to see if he showed up. Bracing a hand against the wall, she eased herself down. She chuckled humorously at the picture she must make. Like a beach ball sitting on top of a flowerpot.

She needed to rest anyway. Everything fatigued her these days. Trying to keep up with twenty grade fivers wore her out but she loved her job. At least her students kept her mind off the fact that she was having a baby soon. Alone.

Phoebe never made a habit of feeling sorry for herself, had prided herself on being strong, facing life head-on. She'd always managed to sound encouraging and supportive when Joshua had prepared to leave on tour again and again. When they'd married, she'd been aware of what she was getting into. So why was the idea of having this baby alone making her come emotionally undone?

Pulling her coat tighter and leaning her head into the corner of the veranda, she closed her eyes. She'd just rest a few minutes.

It was just after dark when Ryan Matthews pulled his sporty compact car into his usual parking spot along the street. It had been drizzling during his entire drive from the hospital. Street lamps lit the area. The trees cast shadows along the sidewalk and even across the steps leading to homes.

He'd had a long day that had involved more than one baby delivery and one of those a tough one. Nothing had seemed to go as planned. Not one but two of the babies had been breech. Regardless, the babies had joined the world kicking and screaming. He was grateful. All the other difficulties seemed to disappear the second he heard a healthy cry. He'd take welcoming a life over dealing with death any day.

Stepping out of the car, he reached behind the driver's seat and grabbed his duffel bag stuffed with his street clothes. Too exhausted to change, he still wore his hospital uniform. As much as he loved his job, thirty-six hours straight was plenty. He was looking forward to a hot shower, bed and the next day off. It would be his first chance in over two weeks to spend time in his workshop. A half-finished chair, along with a table he'd promised to repair for a friend, waited. He wanted to think of nothing and just enjoy the process of creating something with his hands.

Duffel in hand, a wad of dirty uniforms under his arm, he climbed the steps. The light remained on over his door as he'd left it. Halfway up the steps he halted. There was an obviously pregnant woman asleep on his porch. He saw pregnant women regularly in his job as a midwife at Melbourne Victoria Hospital's maternity unit. Today more than he'd wanted to. As if he didn't have a full load at the hospital, they were now showing up on his doorstep.

By the blue tint of the woman's lips and the way she was huddled into a ball, she'd been there for some time. Why was she out in the cold? She should be taking better care of herself, especially at this stage in her pregnancy. Her arms rested on her protruding middle. She wore a fashionable knit cap that covered the top of her head. Strawberry-blond hair twisted around her face and across her shoulders. With the rain and the temperature dropping, she must be uncomfortable.

Taking a resigned breath, Ryan moved farther up the steps. As he reached the top the mysterious woman roused and her eyes popped open. They were large and a dark sable brown with flecks of gold. He'd never seen more mesmerizing or sad ones in his life.

His first instinct was to protect her. He faltered. That wasn't a feeling he experienced often. He made it his practice not to become involved with anyone. Not to care too deeply. He tamped the feeling down. Being tired was all there was to it. "Can I help you?"

The woman slowly straightened. She tugged the not-heavy-enough-for-the-weather coat closer as she stared at him.

When she didn't answer right away he asked in a weary voice, "Do you need help?"

"Are you Ryan Matthews?" Her soft Aussie accent carried in the evening air.

His eyes widened and he stepped back half a

pace, stopping before tumbling. Did he know her? She was such a tiny thing she couldn't be more than a girl. Something about her looked familiar. Could he have seen her in the waiting room sometime?

Ryan glanced at her middle again. He'd always made it a practice to use birth control. Plus, this female was far too young for him. She must be seeking medical help.

"Yes."

"I'm Phoebe Taylor."

Was that supposed to mean something to him? He squinted, studying her face in the dim light. "Have we met before?"

"I should go." She reached out to touch the wall as if she planned to use it as support in order to stand. When she did, a slip of paper fluttered to the stoop.

Ryan picked it up. In blue pen was written his name, address and phone number. Had she been given it at the clinic?

He glared at her. "Where did you get this?"

"I think I had better go." She made a movement toward the steps. "I'm sorry. I shouldn't have come. I'll go."

"I'm afraid I don't understand."

"I don't know for sure what I wanted. I need to go." Her words came out high-pitched and shaky.

He put out a hand as if she were a skittish animal he was trying to reassure. "Think of the baby." That must be what this was all about.

Her eyes widened, taking on a hysterical look. She jerked away from him. "I've done nothing but think of this baby. I have to go. I'm sorry I shouldn't have come." She sniffled. "I don't know…" another louder sniffle "…what I was thinking. You don't know me." Her head went into her hands and she started to cry in earnest. "I'll go. This is…" she sucked in air "…too embarrassing. You must think I'm mad."

He began to think she was. Who acted this way?

She struggled to stand. Ryan took her elbow and helped her.

"I've never done anything…like this before. I need to go."

Ryan could only make out a few of her garbled words through her weeping. He glanced around. If she continued to carry on like this his neighbors would be calling the law.

She shivered. What had she said her name was? Phoebe?

"You need to calm down. Being so upset isn't good for the baby. It's getting cold out and dark. Come in. Let your jacket dry." He needed to get her off the street so he could figure out what this was all about. This wasn't what he had planned for his evening.

"No, I've already embarrassed myself enough. I think I'd better go."

Thankfully the crying had stopped but it had left her eyes large and luminous.

She looked up at him with those eyes laced with something close to pain, and said in a low voice, "You knew my husband."

"Your husband?"

"Joshua Taylor."

Ryan cringed. Air quit moving to his lungs. JT was part of his past. The piece of his life he had put behind him. Ryan hadn't heard JT's name in seven months. Not since he'd had word that he had been killed when his convoy had been bombed.

Why was his wife here? Ryan didn't want to think of the war, or JT. He'd moved on.

They had been buddies while they'd been in Iraq. Ryan had been devastated when he'd heard JT had been killed. He'd been one more in a long list of men Ryan had cared about, shared his life with, had considered family. Now that was gone, all gone. He wasn't going to let himself feel that pain ever again. When he'd left the service he'd promised himself never to let anyone matter that much. He wasn't dragging those ugly memories up for anyone's wife, not even JT's.

Ryan had known there was a wife, had even seen her picture fixed to Joshua's CHU or containerized housing unit room. That had been over five years ago, before he'd left the service. This was his friend's widow?

He studied her. Yes, she did bear a resemblance to the young, bright-faced girl in the pictures. Except that spark of life that had fascinated him back then had left her eyes.

"You need to come in and get warm, then I'll see you get home." He used his midwife-telling-the-mother-to-push voice.

She made a couple of soft sniffling sounds but said no more.

Ryan unlocked the door. Pushing it back, he

offered her space to enter before him. She accepted the invitation. She stopped in the middle of the room as if unsure what to do next. He turned on the light and dropped his bag and dirty clothes in the usual spot on top of all the other dirty clothes lying next to the door.

For the first time, he noted what sparse living conditions he maintained. He had a sofa, a chair, a TV that sat on a wooden crate and was rarely turned on. Not a single picture hung on the walls. He didn't care about any of that. It wasn't important. All he was interested in was bringing babies safely into the world and the saws in his workshop.

"Have a seat. I'll get you some tea," he said in a gruff voice.

Bracing on the arm of the sofa, she lowered herself to the cushion. She pulled the knit cap from her head and her hair fell around her shoulders.

Ryan watched, stunned by the sight. The urge to touch those glowing tresses caught him by surprise. His fingers tingled to test the texture, to see if it was as soft and silky as it looked.

Her gaze lifted, meeting his. Her cheekbones

were high and a touch of pink from the cold made the fairness of her skin more noticeable. Her chin trembled. The sudden fear that she might start crying again went through him. He cleared his throat. "I'll get you that tea."

Phoebe watched as the rather stoic American man walked out of the room. Why had he looked at her that way? Where was all that compassion and caring that Joshua had written about in his letter? Ryan obviously wanted her gone as soon as possible. He wasn't at all what she'd expected. Nothing like Joshua had described him. She shivered, the cold and damp seeping through her jacket. What had she been thinking? This wasn't the warm and welcoming guy that Joshua had said he would be. He hadn't even reacted to her mentioning Joshua.

He was tall, extremely tall. He ducked slightly to go through the doorway. Joshua had been five feet eleven. Ryan Matthews was far taller, with shoulders that went with that height.

Though he was an attractive man with high cheekbones and a straight nose, his eyes held a melancholy gaze. As if he'd seen things and had

had to do things he never wanted to remember, much less talk about.

A few minutes later Ryan handed her a mug with a teabag string hanging over the side. He hadn't even bothered to ask her what she wanted to drink. Did he treat everybody he met with such disinterest?

"I'm a coffee drinker myself. An associate left the tea here or I wouldn't have had it."

She bet it was a female friend. He struck her as the type of man who had women around him all the time. "You are an American."

"Yes."

"Joshua never said that you weren't Australian."

He took a seat in the lone chair in the room. "I guess he didn't notice after a while."

She looked around. Whatever women he brought here didn't stay around long. His place showed nothing of the feminine touch. In fact, it was only just a step above unlivable. If she had to guess, there was nothing but a bed and a carton for a table in the bedroom.

Phoebe watched him drink the coffee, the smell of which wafted her way as she took a sip of her tea.

Quiet minutes later he asked, "How long were you on my doorstep?'

"I don't know. I left home around four."

"It's after seven now." His tone was incredulous. "You've been waiting that long?"

"I fell asleep."

The tension left his face. "That's pretty easy to do in your condition."

"I can't seem to make it without a nap after teaching all day."

"Teaching?"

"I teach at Fillmore Primary School. Grade Five."

He seemed as if he was trying to remember something. "That's right. JT said you were going to school to be a teacher."

At the mention of Joshua they both looked away.

He spoke more to his coffee cup than to her. "I was sorry to hear about Joshua."

"Me, too." He and Joshua were supposed to have been best buddies and that was all he had to say. This guy was so distant he acted as if he'd barely known Joshua. She wouldn't be getting any help or friendship from him.

He looked at her then as if he was unsure about what he might have heard. "Is there something you need from me?"

Phoebe flinched at his directness. Not anymore. She needed to look elsewhere. She wasn't sure what she'd expected from him but this wasn't it. Joshua's letter had assured her that Ryan Matthews would do anything to help her but this man's attitude indicated he wasn't interested in getting involved.

"To tell you the truth, I'm not sure. You were a friend of Joshua's and I just thought…"

"And what did you think? Do you need money?"

"Mr. Matthews, I don't need your money. I have a good job and Joshua's widow and orphans' pension."

"Then I can't imagine what I can do for you, unless you need someone to deliver your baby?"

"Why would I come to you for that?"

"Because I'm a midwife."

"I thought he said you were a medic."

"I was in the army but now I work as a midwife. I still don't understand why you're here. If you need someone to deliver your baby you need to come to the Prenatal Clinic during office hours."

"I already have one. Sophia Toulson."

His brows drew together. "She's leaving soon. Did she send you here?"

She lowered her head.

Had he heard her say, "I just needed a friend, I guess." *A friend?*

He couldn't believe that statement. What kind of person showed up at a stranger's house, asking them to be their friend? Surely she had family and friends in town. Why would she come looking for him now? After all this time. She said she didn't need money so what did she want from him?

"Where's the father of the baby?"

Phoebe sat straighter and looked him directly in the eyes. "Joshua is the father of the baby."

"When...?"

"When he was last home on leave. I wrote to him about the baby but he was..." she swallowed hard "...gone by then." She placed the cup in the crack between the cushions, unable to bend down far enough to put it on the floor. Pushing herself to a standing position, she said, "I think I'd better go."

He glanced out the window. The rain had picked up and the wind was blowing stronger. He huffed as he unfolded from the chair. "I'll drive you home."

"That's not necessary. I can catch the tram."

"Yeah, but you'll get wet getting there and from it to your house. I'll drive you. Where's home?"

Despite his tough exterior, she liked his voice. It was slow, deep and rich. Maybe a Texan or Georgian drawl. "I live in Box Hill."

"That's out toward Ferntree Gully, isn't it?"

"Yes."

"Okay. Let's go."

He sounded resigned to driving her instead of being helpful. This Ryan Matthews didn't seem to care one way or another. Had Joshua gotten him wrong or had Ryan changed?

"If you insist."

"I do." He was already heading toward the door.

"Then thank you."

This trip to see Ryan had been a mistake on a number of levels. But she had learned one thing. She was definitely alone in the world.

* * *

Forty-five minutes later, Ryan pulled onto a tree-lined street with California bungalow-style houses. The lights glowing in the homes screamed warmth, caring and permanency, all the things that he didn't have in his life, didn't want or deserve.

Since they'd left his place Phoebe hadn't tried to make conversation. She'd only spoken when giving him directions. He was no closer than he'd been earlier to knowing what she wanted.

"Next left," she said in a monotone.

He turned there she indicated.

"Last house on the right. The one with the veranda light on."

Ryan pulled his car to the curb. He looked at her house. It appeared well cared-for. A rosebush grew abundantly in the front yard. An archway indicated the main door. The only light shining was the one over it.

"Is anyone expecting you?"

"No."

"You live by yourself?"

"Yes. Did you think I lived with my parents?"

"I just thought since Joshua was gone and you

were having a baby, someone would be nearby. Especially as close as you're obviously getting to the due date."

"No, there's no one. My parents were killed in an auto accident the year before I married. My only brother had moved to England two years before that. We were never really close. There is a pretty large age difference between us." The words were matter-of-fact but she sounded lost.

"Surely someone from Joshua's family is planning to help out?"

"No."

"Really? Why not?"

"If you must know, they didn't want him to marry me. They had someone else picked out. Now that he's gone, they want nothing more to do with me."

"That must have been hard to hear."

"Yeah. It hurt." Her tone said she still was having a hard time dealing with that knowledge. He couldn't imagine someone not wanting to have anything to do with their grandchild.

"Not even the baby?"

She placed her hand on her belly. "Not even the

baby. They told me it would be too hard to look at him or her and know Joshua wasn't here."

"You've got to be kidding!" Ryan's hands tightened on the steering wheel.

"No. That isn't something that I would kid about."

"I'm sorry."

"So am I. But I just think of it as their loss. If that's the way they feel, then it wouldn't ever be healthy for the baby to be around them. We'll be better off without them."

Ryan looked at the house one more time. By its appearance, the baby would be well cared for and loved. "I'll see you to the door."

"That's not necessary." She opened the car door.

He climbed out and hurried around the automobile. She'd started to her feet. He held out a hand. After a second she accepted it. His larger one swallowed her smaller one. Hers was soft and smooth, very feminine. So very different from his. A few seconds later she seemed to gather strength. She removed her hand from his and stood taller.

"Come on, I'll see you to the door." Even to

his own ears it sounded as if he was ready to get rid of her.

"I'll be fine. You've already helped enough by driving me home." She started up the walk lined with flowers and stopped, then looked back at him. "I'm sorry to have bothered you."

Ryan waited to see if she would turn around again, but she didn't. When the light went out on the porch he pulled away from the curb.

Phoebe closed the door behind her with a soft click. Through the small window she saw the lights of Ryan's car as he drove off.

What had she expected? That he would immediately say, "I'll take care of you, I'll be there for you"? She moved through the house without turning any lights on. She knew where every piece of furniture and every lamp was located. With the exception of the few times that Joshua had been home during their marriage, no one had lived with her. Nothing was ever moved unless she did it.

Their marriage had consisted mostly of them living apart. They had met when she was eighteen and fresh out of school. The tall, dark man dressed in a uniform had taken her breath away. Joshua had made it clear what it would be like, being married to a serviceman, and she had been willing to take on that life. She was strong and could deal with it.

It hurt terribly that his parents had said they wouldn't be around to help her with the baby. He or she needed grandparents in their life. With her parents gone they were the only ones. She'd been devastated when she'd received the letter stating they would not be coming around. They had sent some money. Phoebe had thought about returning it but had decided to start a fund at the bank for the baby instead. Not knowing their grandchild would be their loss.

For her the baby was about having a small part of Joshua still in her life. Her hope was that Joshua's parents might change their minds. Either way, right now she was on her own. Not a feeling she enjoyed. In a moment of weakness she'd gone to Ryan's house, but she didn't plan to let him know how bone deep the hurt was that Joshua's parents wanted nothing to do with her. How lonely she was for someone who'd known and loved Joshua.

She turned on the lamp beside her bed and glanced at the picture of her and Joshua smiling. They'd been married eight years but had spent maybe a year together in total. That had been a week or two here, or a month there. They had always laughed that their marriage was like being on vacation instead of the day in, day out experience of living together. Even their jobs had been vastly different. Joshua had found his place in the service more than with her. She'd found contentment in teaching. It had given her the normalcy and stability that being married to a husband who popped in and out hadn't.

Each time Joshua had come home it had been like the first heart-pounding, whirlwind and all-consuming first love that had soon died out and become the regular thud of everyday life. They'd had to relearn each other and getting in the groove had seemed harder to achieve. As they'd grown older they'd both seemed to pull away. She'd had her set life and routine and Joshua had invaded it when he'd returned.

Removing her clothes, she laid them over a chair and pulled her pj's out of the chest of drawers. She groaned. The large T-shirt reminded her of a tent that she and Joshua had camped in just after they'd married. The shirt was huge and still she almost filled it.

Pulling it over her head, she rubbed her belly. The baby had been a complete surprise. She'd given up on ever having children. She and Joshua had decided not to have them since he hadn't been home often enough. She wasn't sure whether or not she'd cared when they'd married or if she'd believed he would leave the army and come home to stay. The idea of having a family had been pushed far into the future. It had become easier just not to consider it. So when she'd come up pregnant it had been a shock.

Her fingers went to her middle, then to her eye, pushing the moisture away. She'd grown up with the dream of having a family one day. Now she was starting a family but with half of it missing.

She pulled the covers back on the bed and climbed in between the cool sheets. Bringing the blanket up around her, she turned on her side, stuffing an extra pillow between the mattress and her tummy. The baby kicked. She laid her hand over the area, feeling the tiny heel that pushed against her side.

The last time Joshua had been home they'd even talked of separating. They'd spent so little time together she'd felt like she hadn't even known her husband anymore. She not only carried Joshua's baby but the guilt that he'd died believing she no longer cared. Friendship had been there but not the intense love that she should have had for a husband.

CHAPTER TWO

THE NEXT MORNING Ryan flipped on the light switch that lit the stairs that led down to his workshop. He'd picked out this town house because of this particular space. Because it was underground it helped block the noise of the saws from the neighbors. The area was also close to the hospital, which made it nice when he had to be there quickly.

Going down the stairs, he scanned the area. A band saw filled one corner, while stationed in the center of the room was a table saw. The area Ryan was most interested in right now was the workbench against the far wall. There lay the half-made chair that he had every intention of finishing today. He would still have to spend another few days staining it.

Picking up a square piece of sandpaper, he began running it up and down one of the curved rockers. He'd made a couple of rockers when the nursery of the hospital had needed new ones. A number of the nurses had been so impressed they'd wanted one of their own. Since then he'd been busy filling orders in his spare time.

Outside the moments when a baby was born and offered its first spirited view of the new world with a shout, being in his shop was the place he was the most happy. Far better than his life in the military.

When he could stand it no longer, he'd resigned his commission. He'd had enough of torn bodies. He ran his hand along the expanse of the wood. It was level but not quite smooth enough. Now he was doing something he loved. But thoughts of Phoebe kept intruding.

He couldn't believe that had been Joshua's wife at his home the night before. Ryan had been living in Melbourne for five years. Joshua had always let him know when he was home, but in all that time he'd never met his wife. It had seemed like his friend's visits had come at the busiest times, and even though the two of them had managed to have a drink together, Ryan had never seen her. Now all of a sudden she had turned up on his doorstep.

Even after he'd gotten her calmed down he hadn't been sure what she'd wanted. It didn't matter. Still, he owed Joshua. He should check on her. But first he'd see what Sophia could tell him.

The next morning, at the clinic, Ryan flipped through his schedule for the day. He had a number of patients to see but none had babies due any time soon. Maybe he would get a few days' reprieve before things got wild again.

"You look deep in thought."

He recognized Sophia's voice and looked up. "Not that deep. You're just the person I wanted to talk to."

The slim woman took one of the functional office chairs in front of his desk. "What can I do for you?"

"I was just wondering what you know about Phoebe Taylor."

"Trying to steal my patients now?" Her eyes twinkled as she asked.

Ryan gave her a dubious look.

She grinned. "She's due in about five weeks. What's happened?"

"She was waiting for me when I got home yesterday. At first I thought she'd gotten my name and address from you. That you were sending her to me because you would be on your honeymoon when it was time to deliver."

Sophia shook her dark-haired head. "Oh, no, it wasn't me. But I remember she mentioned you at one of her appointments and said she had your address."

"I thought maybe she was looking for a midwife. She later told me she was the wife of an army buddy of mine."

"Yes, she told me that you were good friends with her husband. Did she seem okay?"

"Not really. It was all rather confusing and she was quite emotional. I let her get warm, gave her something to drink and took her home."

"She's usually steady as a rock. I'll find out what's going on at her next appointment."

"Thanks, Sophia. I owe her husband."

"I understand. You are coming to my wedding, aren't you?"

Sophia was marrying Aiden Harrison in a few weeks and she wanted everyone there for the event. Ryan wasn't into weddings. He'd never been so close to someone he'd felt like marrying them. After his years in the military he was well aware of how short life could be. Too young to really understand that kind of love when he'd entered the army, he'd soon realized he didn't want to put someone through what Phoebe Taylor had been experiencing.

He didn't understand that type of love. Knew how fleeting it could be. His parents sure hadn't known how to show love. His foster-parents had been poor examples of that also. They had taken care of his physical needs but he'd always been aware that they hadn't really cared about him. The army had given him purpose that had filled that void, for a while. That had lasted for years until the hundreds of faces of death had become heavier with every day. He well understood that losses lasted a lifetime. Even delivering babies and seeing the happiness on families' faces didn't change that. Those men he'd served with were gone. Yet, like JT, they were always with him.

He smiled at Sophia. "I plan to be there. I'll even dust off my suit for the occasion."

"That's great. See you later."

Ryan had seen his last patient for the day and was headed out the glass doors of the Prenatal

Clinic in the hospital. A woman was coming in. He stopped to hold the door for her, then glanced up. It was Phoebe Taylor.

"Ah, hey."

"Hello." Her gaze flicked up at him and then away.

Phoebe must have been coming here for months. How many times had he passed her without having any idea who she was? She looked far less disheveled than she had two days ago. Her hair lay along her shoulders. Dressed in a brown, tan and blue dotted top over brown slacks and low-heeled shoes, she looked professional, classy and fragile.

"Are you looking for me?" Ryan asked.

"I'm here for my appointment with Sophia."

Another mother-to-be came up behind Phoebe. She moved back and out of the way, allowing the woman to go past her. Ryan held the door wide, moving out into the hall. He said to Phoebe, "May I speak to you for a minute?"

A terrified look flicked in her eyes before she gave him a resigned nod. He had the impression that if she could forget they had already met, she'd gladly do so.

Before he could say anything she started, "About the other evening. I'm sorry. I shouldn't have put you on the spot. I had no right to do that."

Here she was the one apologizing and he was the one who should be. "Not a problem. I should have visited you after Joshua died."

Her look was earnest. "That's all right. I understand. Well, I have to get to my appointment."

Apparently whatever she'd needed had been resolved.

"It was nice to meet you, Phoebe."

"You, too." She walked by him, opened the door and went through it. With a soft swish it closed behind her.

Why did he feel as if he needed to say or do more?

Ryan made it as far as his car before curiosity and a nagging guilt caused him to return to the clinic. He waited until Phoebe was finished with her appointment. Phoebe might not agree to him taking her to dinner, but he was going to try. He needed to know why she'd come to see him and even more if there was some way he could help her.

Now that she had contacted him he felt like he owed Joshua that.

On the way to his office he passed a nurse and asked that she let him know when Mrs. Taylor was finished.

Thirty minutes later the nurse popped her head in the door and said Phoebe was on her way out.

Ryan hurried to the waiting room and spotted her as she reached the door. When he called her name she stopped and turned. Her eyes widened in astonishment, then filled with wariness.

"I thought you had left." Phoebe sounded as if she had hoped not to see him again. After his behavior the other night he shouldn't be surprised.

"I came back. I wanted to ask you something."

She raised her brows.

Phoebe wasn't opening the door wide for him. She wouldn't be making this easy.

Thankfully this late in the day the waiting room was empty. "I wondered if I could buy you dinner?"

Phoebe turned her head slightly, as if both studying and judging him. He must have really put her off the other evening. He prided himself on his rapport with people, especially pregnant women and their families. He had let this one down. The guilt he'd felt doubled in size.

"Please. I'd like to make up for how I acted the other night."

"You don't owe me any apologies. I'm the one who showed up on your doorstep unannounced."

"Why don't we both stop taking blame and agree to start again?"

Her eyes became less unsure. "I guess we could do that."

"Then why don't we start by having a burger together?"

"Okay." She agreed with less enthusiasm than he would have liked.

"I know a place just down the street that serves good food. Andrew's Burgers."

"I've heard of it but never been there."

"Great. Do you mind walking?"

"No, I haven't had my exercise today."

Ryan looked at her. If it hadn't been for the baby, she would have been a slim woman. With her coloring she was an eye-catcher, pregnant or not. Her soft, lilting voice was what really caught his attention.

"If you'll wait I'd like to lock up my office."

She nodded. When he returned she was sitting in one of the reclining chairs in the waiting room with her hands resting on the baby.

"I'm ready."

Phoebe looked at him. She pushed against the chair arm to support herself as she stood. "I think this baby is going to be a giant."

"Every mother-to-be that I see thinks that about this time."

As they made their way down the hall to the elevators, Ryan asked, "So how're you and the baby doing?"

A soft smile came to her lips. "Sophia says we're both doing great. I'll have to start coming to clinic every week soon. I just hate that I'm losing her as my midwife. I've become very attached."

"You are getting close."

"I am."

There was depression in her tone that he didn't understand. He knew little about her, but she struck him as someone who would be ecstatic about holding a new life in her hands and caring for someone. Yet he sensed a need in her that he couldn't put a finger on.

They went down the six floors to the lobby of the art deco building and out into the sunlight. The restaurant was a few blocks from the hospital.

"Let's cross the street. I know a shortcut through the park."

She followed him without question. A few minutes later they exited the park and were once again walking along the sidewalk. A couple of times they had to work themselves around other people walking briskly in the opposite direction. Ryan matched his stride to her shorter one and ran interference when someone looked as if they might bump into her.

"I can walk without help, you know."

He glanced at her. She was small but she gave off an air of confidence. It was in complete contrast to her actions that night at his house. Something was going on with her. "I know, but I wouldn't want you to accidentally fall and Sophia would have my head for it."

"I think they gave up chopping off heads in Australia a long time ago," she said in a dry tone.

"Still, I'm kind of scared of Sophia. I don't know if I could face her if I let you get hurt."

That got a smile out of her. "Here we are," Ryan said as he pulled the glass door of the restaurant open and allowed Phoebe to enter ahead of him.

She wasn't sure sharing a meal with Ryan was such a good idea. He'd asked nicely enough and she hadn't eaten out in so long she hadn't had the heart to say no. She suspected either his curiosity or some kind of obligation he felt toward Joshua had made him ask. No way had he changed overnight into being the emotional support she'd naively hoped he might be. A nice meal shared with someone was all she expected to get out of the next hour.

When Ryan was asked if they wanted a booth or table he glanced at her middle and grinned. He had a wide smile and nice even teeth. "I guess we'd better go for a table."

They were directed to one. The restaurant was decorated in a 1950s diner style, all chrome, red-covered chairs and white tile on the floor. Lighting hung over each booth and table. It was still early for the dinner crowd so it wasn't noisy. Phoebe wasn't sure if she considered that good or bad.

She took a seat. Ryan sat in the chair across the table from her.

"So I need to order a hamburger, I'm thinking." Phoebe took the menu out of the metal rack on the table.

"They have good ones. But there are also other things just as good."

The waitress arrived and took their drink order. Phoebe opened a menu but Ryan didn't. When the waitress returned with their glasses, she asked what they would like to order. Phoebe decided on the burger without onions and Ryan ordered his with everything.

The waitress left and Ryan asked, "No onions?"

"They don't agree with me."

"That's typical. I know a mother who said she couldn't cook bacon the entire first three months of her pregnancy."

"Smells used to bother me but that has become better."

Ryan crossed his arms and leaned on the table. "So do you know if it's a boy or a girl?"

"I don't know."

"Really?"

Phoebe almost laughed at his look of shock. "Don't want to know. I like surprises."

"That's pretty amazing in this day and age where everyone is wanting to know the sex and you don't. I wouldn't want to know, either. One of my favorite moments during a delivery is the look on the parents' faces when they discover the sex."

Phoebe got the impression that she'd gone up a notch in his estimation.

"You know, I don't know any other male midwife."

"There are only a few of us around. More in Australia than in the US."

"So why did you become one?"

"I wanted to do something that made me smile." He picked up his drink. "I was tired of watching people's lives being destroyed or lost when I was in the service. I wanted to do something that involved medicine but had a happy ending. What's better than bringing a life into the world?"

He was right. What was better than that?

The waitress brought their meals. They didn't speak for a while.

It fascinated Phoebe that they were virtual

strangers but seem to be content sharing a meal together. This evening stood in sharp contrast to when they had met. Being around this Ryan put her at ease for some reason. After their first meeting she would have sworn that couldn't be possible.

She ate half her burger and chips before pushing them aside.

"You're eating for two, you know," Ryan said with a raised brow.

"The problem is that when this baby comes I don't want to look like I ate for three." She wiped her mouth with her napkin and placed it on the table.

"How's your weight gain?"

Phoebe leaned back in her chair. "That's certainly a personal question."

"I'm a midwife. I ask that question all the time."

"Yes, but you aren't my midwife."

He pushed his empty plate away. "I'll concede that. But I'm only asking out of concern."

"If it'll make you feel better my weight is just fine. I'm within the guidelines."

"Good. You look like you're taking care of yourself."

"I try to eat right and get some exercise every day." She looked pointedly at her plate. "Not that this burger was on the healthy chart."

He shrugged. "No, it probably isn't, but every once in a while it's okay."

They lapsed into silence again as the waitress refilled their glasses and took away their plates.

A few minutes later Phoebe said, "I know this might be tough but I was wondering if you might be willing to tell me some stories about Joshua. Something I could tell the baby. Something about him outside of just what I remember."

Ryan's lips tightened and he didn't meet her gaze.

"You don't have to if you don't want to."

After a moment he met her look. "What would you like to know?"

"I guess anything. I feel like you knew him better than me. You spent far more time together than we did. I was wondering how you met?"

Ryan's gray eyes took on a faraway look. "The Aussie and the US troops didn't always hit it off, but JT and I did. We didn't usually work together, but I was asked to go out on patrol with his platoon. Their medic was on leave and the replacement hadn't made it in yet. My commander agreed. It was supposed to be an easy in and out of a village under our control. All went well until we were headed out, then all hell broke loose. The Iraqis had us pinned down and we couldn't expect help until the next morning.

"A couple of JT's men were seriously injured. While we spent long hours hunkered down together we got to know each other pretty well. He told me about you, and I told him about growing up in Texas.

"When I told him that I was tired of having to patch up people that another human had destroyed, he encouraged me to do something different. Even suggested I move to Australia for a new start. He joked that if he ever left the army he'd use his skills to become a police officer."

Phoebe had never heard Joshua say anything about wanting to do that. He had told Ryan things he either hadn't wanted to share with her or couldn't. It made her sad and angry at the same time. She and Joshua had just not been as close as a married couple should have been.

"After that kind of night you know each other pretty well. We started getting together for drinks whenever we had leave at the same time." His eyes didn't meet hers. "JT found out that I didn't get much mail so he shared his letters with me."

For seconds Phoebe panicked, trying to remember what she had said in her letters. Misery overtook the panic. During the last few years of their marriage her letters had been less about them personally and more about what was happening with her students, how Melbourne was changing, what she was doing at the house. It had been as if she'd been writing to a friend instead of her husband.

"I always looked forward to your letters. They were full of news and I liked to hear about your class. The letters your students wrote were the best. There was something about them that helped make all the ugliness disappear for a while."

"I'm glad they helped. My students liked writing them. Thank you for telling me about Joshua. I guess I just wanted to talk about him. This is his baby and he isn't around. Just hearing about him makes him seem a little closer. But it's time for me to go." She needed to think about what Ryan had told her. The fact that someone had known her husband better than she had made her feel heartsick.

Ryan stood and Phoebe did also. She led the way to the door. Outside Ryan turned in the direction of the hospital.

"I need to go this way to catch the tram. Thanks for dinner." She turned toward the left.

"I'll give you a ride home," Ryan said.

"I don't want you to drive all the way out to my house."

"I don't mind and you don't need to be so late getting home. Don't you own a car?"

"No, I can take the tram to almost anything I need."

"But you're making two-hour round trips to see Sophia. In America we can't live without a car. There isn't public transportation everywhere."

"Yes, but that's only once a month and it's worth it to have Sophia as my midwife. I wish she was going to be there for the delivery."

"I realize that I live in Australia, but I can't get used to prenatal care being called antenatal. It took me forever to tell the mothers I saw that they needed to come to the antenatal clinic. I just think prenatal."

"The ideas and ways we grow up with are hard to change."

"Yes, once an idea gets fixed in my head it's hard to make me budge. And with that thought, not to make you feel bad, but you look like you could use some rest. I'm driving you home."

"I am tired and I know now that you won't change your mind. I'm going to accept the ride."

"Good."

Ryan escorted Phoebe back to the hospital and to his car. The sidewalk wasn't near as busy as it had been earlier. It had been a long time since he'd done something as simple as stroll through a park with a woman. He couldn't remember ever doing so with one who was expecting. People smiled and greeted Phoebe. She returned them. A number of times they turned to him and offered their congratulations. The first time he began to explain but soon realized it was a waste of time. Instead, he nodded noncommittally.

"I'm sorry," Phoebe said after the first incident.

"Not your fault. You can't help what they think."

He had hardly pulled out of the parking area before Phoebe had closed her eyes. She was tired.

Ryan got a number of reactions when he told someone he was a midwife. He'd gotten used to it. But the one thing he couldn't get used to was not being able to understand all the nuances of the female body when a baby was growing inside it. The sudden ability to go to sleep anywhere and in any position was one of those. It must be like being in the army. He had learned to sleep anywhere at any time.

Phoebe blinked with the small jolt of the car stopping. She'd fallen asleep again. It was getting embarrassing.

"I'm sorry. I didn't mean to go to sleep."

"Not a problem. You're not the first woman I've put to sleep."

Phoebe gave him a questioning look. She bet she wasn't. What had her thinking of Ryan in that suggestive way?

"I'm the one sorry this time. I didn't mean it like that."

"Like what?" She gave him her best innocent look.

"You know, like…"

Phoebe enjoyed his flustered expression and the pinkness that began to work its way up his neck.

She rested her hands on each side of her belly. "I'm well aware of the facts of life and how a man can satisfy a woman."

He grinned. "You're laughing at me now."

Phoebe chuckled. "I guess I am." She opened her car door. "Thanks for the burger and the ride. Also thanks for telling me about Joshua. You have no idea how much it means to me."

"Hey, wait a minute."

Before she could get completely out of the car Ryan had come round and was standing on the path, reaching to help her. His hand went to her elbow and he supported her as she stood. He pushed the door closed behind her and it made a thud.

"Listen, if there's anything that I can do for you..."

He sounded sincere. "I appreciate it... Uh, there is one thing I could use some help with."

"What's that?"

His voice held an eager tone as if he was looking for a chance to atone for his earlier behavior. She hated to ask him but couldn't think of another way to get it done before the baby came. "I had a bed for the baby delivered but it needs to be put together. I would pay you."

Ryan looked as if she had slapped him. "You will not. How about I come by Saturday afternoon? If I have to work I'll call and let you know, otherwise I'll be here on Saturday."

"Thank you, that would be wonderful." And she meant it. She'd spent more than one night worrying over how she was going to get that baby bed assembled.

"Not a problem. Do you have tools or do I need to bring mine?"

"You might want to bring yours. I have a few but only necessities like a hammer and screwdriver."

"Then it's a plan. Why don't you give me your number?" Ryan took out his cellphone and punched in the numbers she told him.

"I'll be here after lunch on Saturday, unless you hear differently from me."

"Thank you."

"No worries. Furniture I can do."

Something about Ryan made her believe that

he had many talents if he was just willing to show them.

"Come on. I'll walk you to your door."

Phoebe didn't argue this time.

"See you Saturday." With that he turned and left her to enter her home.

She was putting her key in the lock when she noticed the curtain of her neighbor's house flutter. Mrs. Rosenheim had been watching. She would no doubt be over the next afternoon to get all the particulars about who Ryan was and how Phoebe knew him.

Ryan was as good as his word. He was there on Saturday just after lunchtime with a tool bag in his hand. Mrs. Rosenheim was sitting at Phoebe's kitchen table when the knock came at the door.

"I won't stay but I am going to check this boy out before I go."

Phoebe would have argued but it wouldn't have done her any good. Despite the fact that Mrs. Rosenheim was probably older than Phoebe's grandmother would be, she was a commanding presence and was only concerned for Phoebe's welfare. They had started taking care of each other two years ago when Phoebe had moved in.

Joshua had only been home once since she'd been living there. He'd not been impressed with Mrs. Rosenheim, calling her the "old busybody bird." Phoebe had learned to appreciate her concern. If nothing else, she knew someone would miss her if she didn't come home.

She opened the door for Ryan. "Come in."

"How're you doing?"

The question sounded like he was making pleasant conversation, but he was also looking at her with a trained eye. He smelled of sawdust with a hint of citrus. It made her want to step closer. Take a deeper breath.

"I'm feeling fine." She smiled and he nodded.

"Good. I told Sophia that I would check."

Mrs. Rosenheim shuffled into the room.

Ryan looked from her to Phoebe. "Ryan, this is my neighbor, Mrs. Rosenheim."

He sat his tool bag on the floor at his feet and extended a hand. "Nice to meet you."

"You're American."

"Yes, ma'am. Texan."

Mrs. Rosenheim made a noncommittal sound

low in her throat. Ryan gave Phoebe a questioning look. She shrugged her shoulders.

"So you knew Mr. Taylor."

A guarded look came over Ryan's face. "Yes, JT and I served in Iraq together."

"Bad thing, leaving Phoebe here all by herself all the time. A man should want to be at home with his wife. She needs someone to watch over her. Help her."

Phoebe didn't miss the color wash out of Ryan's face.

"It was his job. The army," Phoebe said quietly.

"I know, sweetie. But a woman not only wants a man to help put a roof over her head but to be around when the times are hard." She directed the last few words at Ryan.

"Uh, Mrs. Rosenheim, I think we need to let Ryan get started on the bed. I'm sure he has other places he needs to go today." Phoebe shook her head at him when she started to say something.

"I'm next door if you need me." Mrs. Rosenheim made her way out with a last glance at Ryan.

"Formidable lady," Ryan said with a grin.

"Yes. She and Joshua didn't like each other on

sight, but she's been good to me. She was with the men who came from the military department to tell me about Joshua. I don't know what I would have done without her shoulder to cry on. She's also the one who realized I was pregnant when I started being sick."

Phoebe suddenly needed to focus on something else. She shook away the memories. Ryan was the first male to have come into her home in over a year. He seemed to take up the entire space. "Anyway, let me show you where the bed is."

Ryan followed Phoebe down a hallway that had four doors leading off of it. She stopped at the next to last one and nudged the door open.

Against one wall was a large brown box that Ryan guessed was the baby bed. That didn't surprise him. What did were the piles of books stacked around the room and the desk painted in a folk art style with a chair of the same kind sitting in one corner. The walls were painted a dark gray. Two cans of paint sat in another corner. He fully expected to see a room decorated in all the frills and with toys waiting for a baby. He'd listened to enough mothers talk about what they had done in the baby's room or were going to do to know that Phoebe was far behind in her preparations.

She placed her hand on the box. "This is the bed."

"Great. I'll get it put together."

Walking to the door, she looked back at him. "You didn't have to agree to this, but I really appreciate you doing it."

"Not a problem."

He'd been working for an hour when Phoebe returned to stand in the doorway. His back was to her but he felt her presence.

"I brought you something to drink." She moved to the desk and placed the drink on it.

Ryan stood from where he'd been tightening a screw on the back of the bed. He picked up the glass, took a long swallow of water and put it back on the desk again.

Phoebe had an odd look on her face that quickly disappeared.

Ryan said, "I guess I'm doing pretty well. I don't think I'm going to have but two screws and one thingamajig left over."

She laughed.

Had he ever heard anything more beautiful? It was almost musical. He vowed then to give her a reason to laugh often.

"My father always said that if you didn't have parts left over then you didn't put it together correctly."

"Where did you grow up?"

"In a small town about fifty miles from here."

"Is that where you met JT?"

"Yeah. We had a military base nearby. I worked at a local restaurant and Joshua and some of his mates came in for dinner one night and sat at my table."

"And, as they say, the rest was history."

"Yes, it was. I was wondering if…uh, you might like to stay for dinner? I do most of my cooking on the weekends so that I don't have to stand up any more than necessary during the week. How do grilled lamb chops with three vegetables sound?"

When had been the last time he'd eaten a home-cooked meal? Ryan couldn't remember. He grabbed what he did eat from the hospital cafeteria or from a fast-food place. The thought of sitting down to a real meal was more than he could resist. "That sounds great."

"Good. Then I'll go finish up."

She'd already moved to leave when he said, "Phoebe, I couldn't help but notice that you don't have this room set up for a baby."

Making a slow turn, she faced him. "I don't need you to make me feel ashamed. I bet you think I sank so far into feeling sorry for myself that I didn't pay attention to getting ready for the baby. I was still in shock over Joshua when I found out I was pregnant. I just couldn't bring myself to do anything for a while. Anyway, it has been pushed back. Maybe I'll have time to do something after the baby comes."

That wasn't going to happen. Ryan had also heard the new mothers talking about how they never got anything done any more. "I didn't mean to make you feel ashamed or defensive. I was thinking I could help. I see you have paint. How about letting me do the walls for you? I could also move this desk and chair to where you want it and the books."

"I hate to have you do all that."

"I don't mind. All you'd have to do is tell me where to put everything."

She rested her hand on her middle. A wistful look came to her eyes. "It would be nice to have the room ready for the baby. I had planned to buy some stuff for the walls."

"We could do that together." It was the least he could do for Joshua. This was practical stuff that needed doing. He had a strong back and could take care of them. He couldn't fix the fact she was having this baby all by herself but he could help with the everyday aspects of adding a new person to her household.

"That sounds like I'm asking too much."

"You're not asking. I volunteered. I'd like to do it. If JT were here, he'd be doing it. This will be my way of helping him out, like he did me."

Her eyes darkened for a second and then she nodded. "Then thanks. I'll gladly accept your help, but I'm going to warn you that you may wish you hadn't."

"How's that?"

"I have so many ideas for this room you'll get tired of me telling you what to do."

"We'll see. I'll be through here in about ten

minutes, then I'd like to get started on the painting. Do you have any paint supplies?"

"They're in the shed in the backyard. When you get done, come to the kitchen and I'll take you out and show you where they are."

"Will do."

He watched her leave. Even with the bulk she carried she had a graceful stride. What had possessed him to get this caught up in doing a baby's room? He made a practice of not getting involved.

Guilt, pure and simple.

CHAPTER THREE

PHOEBE HAD SPENT so much time without a man
or his help it made her nervous to have Ryan in
her house. While he'd been putting together the
bed, she'd been in the kitchen, cooking. Still,
she'd been aware of every clatter or thump that
had come from the direction of the bedroom. On
occasion she'd heard a swear word. She smiled.
More than once her father had bloodied his
knuckles, putting a toy together for her or her
brother.

It was nice to have someone in the house. She'd
considered getting a dog or cat a couple of times
just so there would be a living, breathing thing
around. She'd decided to wait because she didn't
want the poor animal alone in the house all day.

Ryan came around the corner. "All done. Come
see what you think."

She put the plate on the table and headed down
the hall, well aware of him following her. He'd

pushed the bed up against the wall across from the window. It looked like the perfect place for it. She ran her hand along the railing. "It looks wonderful."

"Do you have a mattress for it?"

"Yes, it's in the other bedroom."

"I'll get it."

He soon returned with a mattress covered in protective plastic. Together they worked to remove it. Ryan lifted the bedding and dropped it into place.

"It almost makes it real," she said with a note of wonder.

"What?"

"A baby coming."

He chuckled. "I would think that large mound you're sporting out front would make it seem pretty real."

"It does but the bed is something tangible."

"What about a rocker or any other furniture?"

She shrugged. "I'll have to go buy something. I was hoping I could find some pieces at a garage sale that I could redo. I wanted to paint it bright and add animals and plants, that sort of thing."

"You mean like the other folk art you have in the living room?"

She looked at him with a brightness that said they were talking about a passion of hers. "You know about folk art?"

"Only what it is. I'm more a straight paint and stain kind of guy. Fancy painting isn't my thing. So, if you'll show me where you want these books, I'll start moving them."

"They go in my bedroom."

She went out the doorway and turned toward the end of the hall, then went through an open doorway. Ryan followed more slowly. Why did it bother him that he had just been invited into his buddy's wife's bedroom? She hadn't even thought about what she was saying. When she looked back he was standing in the doorway.

"They go on this bookshelf. If you'll bring them to me, I can shelve them."

Ryan returned with an armload of books. She'd taken a seat on the floor in front of the shelving while he'd been gone.

He stacked the books on the floor and she went to work, putting them in place.

* * *

Ryan looked down at Phoebe. He saw pregnant women day in and day out, but there was something almost angelic about the way her golden hair covered a portion of her face and her small hands put the books so neatly into their spots.

He shook his head and strode toward the door. Had he been spending too much time in his shop alone? The sawdust was filling his brain.

Fifteen minutes later he had all the books moved. Phoebe hadn't worked as fast as he so she was still shelving books. Not wanting to sit on her bed, he stood near the door until she was finished.

"Thanks for doing this. I've been dreading it for weeks. That's why it hasn't been done." She continued to work.

Ryan's cell phone rang and he pulled it out of his pocket. "I have to get this."

She nodded.

"Ryan Matthews."

"It's Julie Habershire. My waters just broke."

"Okay. No need to panic. We talked about what to do if this happens. I'll meet you at the hospital. Drive safe."

"Ryan, the baby will be all right, won't it? It's early."

"The baby should be fine. Not so early it shouldn't be perfect. See you soon."

He touched the phone to disconnect the call. Phoebe looked at him with a slight smile on her face. "Are you always that calm and reassuring with your patients?"

"I try to be."

"That's a special gift."

"I just know that people are scared when they have never experienced something before, especially if it has to do with their bodies. I learned a long time ago if I don't sound upset, then they're more likely not to get upset."

"You must be good at your job."

He slipped the phone back into his pocket. "I hope my patients think so. Anyway, I've got to go. I hate to miss out on that meal, but babies don't wait."

"I understand."

"Would it be all right if I come back tomorrow and get started on that painting? Maybe get in on leftovers?"

"That sounds fine to me. After lunch?"

"Then it's a plan. See you then." He turned to head out the door and stopped. Coming back, he offered her his hand. "If I don't help you up, I'm afraid you might still be on the floor when I return tomorrow."

"Are you implying that I'm so big that I can't get up off the floor by myself?" She accepted his hand. He helped her rise. She did it with grace.

With her on her feet, he put up his hands as if defending himself. "Hey, I work with pregnant women every day and I know better than to do that. Have to go. See you later."

Her soft laugh followed him down the hall. He went out the front door with a grin on his face, something he'd done more in the last few days than he had in years.

The next afternoon Phoebe wasn't sure what was happening but she was going to take Ryan's help while it was being offered. She'd sat around for too long with no direction. Well aware that she needed to be getting the baby's room together, she hadn't had the heart to do so. It was just too sad to work on it by herself. Having the bed assembled made her want to do more. It needed sheets, blankets. There should be other pieces of furniture, pictures on the walls.

Next weekend she'd go to some garage sales and see if she could find a few items. She smiled. For once she was feeling some excitement over the prospect of being a mother. For now she'd be satisfied with just having the room painted.

She'd hardly finished her lunch sandwich when there was a knock at the door. Ryan stood there. Dressed in cargo pants and a white T-shirt that hugged his well-defined physique, he was a fine-looking man. Mrs. Rosenheim had made a point to tell Phoebe the same thing that morning. Ryan proved that just because she was pregnant it didn't mean that she couldn't be affected by a man. It took her time to draw enough breath to say hello.

"Hey," he said in that drawl that left her feeling like she was sitting beside a cool stream on a hot summer day. "How about showing me the paint supplies? If I need anything I'll still have time to go to the store before it closes."

"Okay. It's this way." This was the first time he hadn't taken time to ask her how she was doing. He seemed focused on the project. She kind of liked the fact that he didn't see her as only a pregnant woman.

At the shed, she started to raise the roll-top door. Ryan stopped her by placing his hand over hers. His hand wasn't smooth, like she had expected for a midwife. Instead, it had a coarseness to it that spoke of a man who did more than wear gloves all the time.

"Hey, you don't need to be doing that. Let me get it."

What would have taken her great effort seemed as easy for him as lifting a blind.

"The paint stuff is stacked up over there." She pointed to the right and toward the back of the shed.

"I see it." He leaned over some gardening pots to gather the items, while at the same time presenting her with a nice view of his behind.

"Would you mind carrying a couple of things?"

It took her a second to answer. "No."

Ryan looked over his shoulder and gave her a speculative look. "Here." He handed her a few brushes and a package of rollers, then came out holding an armload of drop cloths and a paint tray. "I think this is everything I need."

They walked back to the house. Phoebe held the door open for him to enter. He was laying supplies on the floor of the baby's room by the time she entered. He took what she carried from her and added them to the pile.

Scanning the room, he said, "Is the desk staying in here?"

She looked at it. Ryan's drive to get things done was surpassing what she had thought through. "I had planned to put it in the living room. But I'll need to move a few things around so it'll have a place. Give me a minute and I'll see what I can do."

"You're not moving anything by yourself."

Phoebe faced him with her hands on her hips. "I appreciate your help. Really I do, but up until a few days ago I had no help. No one telling me what I should and shouldn't do. I am fully capable of moving a few things. If it's too large for me to do so, I'll call you."

Ryan's look met hers. He pursed his lips. She'd got his attention.

"I'm sorry. I stepped over the line, didn't I?"

She nodded. "Yes. Just a little bit."

"Then please let me know if and when you need help." He bowed slightly.

"Thank you. I will." She left the room with her head held high. She was grateful for Ryan's help but she wasn't needy, despite what her behavior at his house had implied.

In the living room, she began moving small items off an end table. Ryan's soft whistle drifted up the hall. It was nice to have someone around. Her smile grew. It would be nice to have a baby in the house.

She had reached to move the end table when behind her came, "I knew I couldn't trust you."

Jerking to a standing position, she looked around to find Ryan standing with his shoulder leaning against the wall.

"Are you checking up on me?"

"Do you need to be checked up on?"

"No." The word didn't come out as confidently as she would have liked.

He came toward her. "I think you might." He placed his hands on the table and looked at her. "Where do you want this?"

She pointed to the other end of the sofa, where she'd cleared a space by moving a floor lamp.

Ryan moved the table into the spot. He ran a finger over a painted swirl on it. "This type of artwork is interesting."

"Thank you."

He looked at her. "You did this?"

"Don't act so surprised."

"I didn't mean it like that." He looked around the room. "You did all of this?"

She stood straighter. "I did, even down to making the cushions and curtains."

"I'm impressed. I like it."

She chuckled dryly. "Now I'm surprised. Joshua hated this type of decorating. He said it made us look like we couldn't afford better. I put most of it away when he came home. Pulled it out again when he had gone again."

Ryan looked at her for a long moment. "Well, I like it. It's you."

She didn't think anyone had said anything nicer to her in a long time. "Thank you. I appreciate that."

"You're welcome. Now, if I go paint another wall, can I trust you to behave?"

Phoebe glared at him. "Yes, I'll put our supper on to warm. Will that make you happy?"

"Yes." With that, he went off whistling down the hall.

Half an hour later Phoebe went to check on Ryan's progress. He was getting ready to start on the last wall. The others were already a pale yellow. A cheerful and happy color.

The room was small but he seemed very efficient. She watched as he bent to apply paint to the roller in the tray. The muscles on his back rippled. He reached up and brought the roller down along the wall. His biceps flexed and released.

Phoebe shook her head. She had been without a man for far too long and yet was far too pregnant to consider having a relationship with one now. Still, she was alive…

Ryan turned. By the look in his eyes and the way he watched her like a cat after a bird, he knew what she'd been doing. She'd never been much of a blusher but she felt the heat rising to her face.

"So what do you think?"

Thankfully he hadn't made a comment about her staring. "It looks beautiful."

"The paint goes on great."

She stepped farther into the room. "This isn't your first time to do this."

"No. My foster-father was a painter. I started working with him when I was fourteen." He moved back to filling the roller again.

Phoebe wasn't sure she should ask but she was too curious not to. "You were a foster-child?"

"Yeah. I never knew my father and my mother was a drug addict. I was five when I was taken away from her."

Her heart hurt for that little boy. "Oh, Ryan."

He shrugged. "It was tough but it was a long time ago."

Something about his attitude told her it still affected him. His focus turned to refilling the roller again.

"So your foster-father let you go to work with him?"

"It was more like made me go. I was a difficult teen and he thought it would help keep me in line. Something about idle hands leaving room for trouble."

"And did it keep you in line?"

"Not really. I ended up going into the army the

day after I graduated from high school. It made my foster-parents happy, and me, too."

"Even your foster-mother?"

He glanced back at her. "She didn't mind, either. She was so exhausted from dealing with the smaller kids and my behavior she was glad to see me go. I should be finished here in about thirty minutes. Any chance I could get something to eat?"

He was apparently through discussing his childhood. She would see to it that her child felt loved and wanted. "It'll be ready."

Ryan washed up in the hall bathroom. Splashing water on his face, he looked into the mirror. What was he doing? He could feel himself getting in too deep. He'd enjoyed the afternoon more than he would have ever imagined. He spent most of his off hours in his shop and he found he rather liked being out in the daylight, spending time with someone.

He entered the kitchen. There he found more of the same decor as the rest of the house. The table had four chairs, each painted a different color yet they seem to complement each other. The eclectic look seemed to suit Phoebe.

The table was set. When was the last time he'd eaten dinner off something other than a takeout plate?

"You may sit there." Phoebe pointed to the chair closest to him and turned back to the oven. She pulled out a casserole pan and placed it in the center of the table.

Ryan leaned in close and inhaled. "Smells wonderful."

He didn't miss her pleased smile. Phoebe would make a great mother. She found pleasure in doing for others.

She handed him a serving spoon. "Help yourself."

Ryan didn't need to be told twice. He scooped two large helpings onto his plate. Phoebe took one. When she picked up her fork, he did also.

"I see you were taught manners. Not eating until everyone else does."

"My foster-mother was a real stickler about them." He put a forkful into his mouth. It was the best thing he'd eaten in years. "This is good. Real good."

"Thank you. It's my grandmother's chicken casserole recipe."

He ate a plateful and one more before he sat back and looked at Phoebe. She had only eaten about half of what she'd put on her plate.

"You need to eat more."

She looked down at her middle. "I don't think I need to get any bigger."

"You look wonderful."

"You are feeding me compliments now."

Ryan chuckled. "That wasn't my intent. But I guess I am."

"I'll take them any way I can get them." It was nice to be noticed by a male on any level.

Ryan pushed his chair back. "I guess I'd better get the paint supplies cleaned up."

He left and she cleared the table. When done, she went to see if she could help Ryan. He was in the process of moving the desk.

"That's heavy. Let me help you."

Ryan jerked around. "You will not."

"There's no way you can move that desk by yourself."

"It's all in the technique." He gripped it by each

side and began walking it from one corner to the other until he'd moved it to the doorway.

"Do you have an old towel I can use?" Ryan asked.

"Just a second." Phoebe went into the bathroom and brought back the largest one she could find. She handed it to Ryan.

"You stay out here." He moved the desk out into the hall. Taking the towel, he laid it on the floor in front of the desk. Lifting one end he asked, "Can you put the towel under the desk as far as possible?"

Glad she could be of some help she did as he requested.

He then lowered the desk. "Perfect." Gathering the corners of the towel into his hands he slowly pulled the desk over the wooden flooring and down the hall.

Phoebe stepped into the doorway, letting him pass. When he was by, she stepped out and began to push.

Coming to a stop, Ryan growled, "What're you doing?"

"Helping."

"You shouldn't—"

"Stop telling me what to do. I'm not really doing much."

A grunt of disbelief came from his direction but the desk started moving again. She continued to help maneuver it, seeing that it didn't nick the walls or hit any other furniture. When the desk quit moving, she looked over it. Her gaze met Ryan's. For a second his intense gray gaze held hers. Warmth washed over her. Could he see things she'd rather keep hidden?

"Why did you stop?"

His mouth quirked. "I don't know where you want this."

Phoebe tried to squeeze through the space between the desk and the wall.

"Hold on a sec and let me move it." Ryan grabbed the desk and shifted it so she could join him.

"I want it put over there." She pointed to the space she had cleared under a window.

"Okay." He began walking and shifting the desk until it was in place. "I'll go get the chair." He left.

The desk really needed to be centered under

the window. Phoebe placed one hip against the side and pushed. It only moved a few centimeters.

"I can't leave you alone for a minute." Ryan's deep voice came from behind her.

"It needs to be centered under the window."

"Then why didn't you say something?"

He put his hands on her waist or what had once been her waist. Her breath caught. Ryan gently directed her out of the way, then quickly put space between them. "I'm sorry. I shouldn't have done that."

Ryan acted as if he'd been too personal with her. "It's okay," she said.

"Stand over there, out of the way, and tell me when I have it where you want it."

"You do know I'm just pregnant, not an invalid."

He gave her a pointed look. "I'm well aware of that but some things you shouldn't be doing, whether you're pregnant or not. This is one of them. Now, tell me where you want it."

Shifting the desk an inch, he looked at her for confirmation. It still wasn't where she wanted it. "Move it to the right just a little."

Had he muttered "Women" under his breath?

"That's it. Perfect. Thank you."

He stood and rubbed his lower back.

She stepped closer. "Did you hurt yourself?"

He grinned. "No. I was just afraid that you might ask me to move something else."

"Hey, you're the one who volunteered."

"That I did. I might ought to think about it before I do that again." He continued stretching.

"Might ought to?" She liked his accent.

"Ought to. Texas. Southern. Ought to go. Ought to get."

Phoebe laughed. "I'll have to remember that. Use it sometime."

"I think you ought not make fun of me."

"And I think you ought not be so sensitive."

They both laughed.

It was the first real laugh she'd shared with someone in a long time. It felt good.

"Well, I guess I had better go. It's getting late."

"I really appreciate all your work today. The baby's room looks wonderful. I can hardly wait to go to some garage sales and look for a chest of drawers."

"And how do you plan to get something like that home?"

"I'll worry about that if I find one. Some people are willing to deliver if I ask."

"I don't have any mothers due for a couple of weeks so why don't I go with you on Saturday?"

She like the idea but didn't want to take advantage of him. "I hate to take up another one of your weekends."

"I'd like to go. I've got a buddy who has a truck and lets me borrow it sometimes."

The truck was a plus and it would be nice to have company. "I won't turn that down."

"Great. I'll be here early Saturday to pick you up."

Ryan headed out the front door. "See you then."

"Bye." Phoebe watched from the veranda as Ryan drove away. She could get used to having him around. Seeing him on Saturday gave her something to look forward to. Of course she appreciated his help but more than that she liked him. There was an easy way about him that made life seem like fun. She was far too attracted to him already. Joshua had been right about him. Maybe she had found someone she could depend on.

Warmth lingered where Ryan had touched her.

A ripple of awareness had gone up her spine. What was she thinking? Joshua had been dead for less than a year and she had a baby on the way, and here she was mooning over Ryan.

Still, Saturday couldn't come soon enough.

CHAPTER FOUR

RYAN PULLED THE truck to the curb in front of Phoebe's house just as the sun became warm.

What was he doing? The question kept rotating through his mind like a revolving door. He was too interested in Phoebe. But it was hard not to be. Those large, vulnerable eyes drew him in. Still, he admired the way she had stood up to him when he'd stepped over the line to bossing her around. The brief moments he'd touched her waist had told him that he could want more than just to help her. That wasn't going to happen. Still, he'd looked forward to spending the day with her.

Phoebe met him halfway up the walk. She wore jeans and a simple white shirt. Her eyes sparkled and for a woman of her size she walked with a peppy step. A smile covered her face. She reminded him of springtime. A fresh start.

If he'd seen any woman look more alluring, he couldn't remember when. "Mornin'."

"Hi. You ready to go? We need to get going. You know the early bird gets the worm." She carried a newspaper and passed him on the way to the truck, leaving the smell of flowers swirling in the air. He was tempted to breathe deeply. Let his mind commit it to memory.

"Uh…yeah. I'm ready." Ryan wasn't able to keep the astonishment out of his voice. He hurried to join her. Phoebe was a woman on a mission.

She had climbed into the passenger seat and closed the door before he reached the truck. He took his place behind the wheel. "So where's the fire?"

"What?" She looked up from the open paper.

"What's the hurry?"

"I think they have just what I need at a sale and I don't want it to get bought up before we get there."

"Why didn't you call me? I could have come earlier."

"I didn't know for sure until I phoned a few

minutes ago. They wouldn't promise to hold it for me so we've got to go."

Ryan grinned as he pulled away from the curb. There was nothing like a woman looking for a deal. "So where are we headed?"

"South. It's about forty minutes away." Phoebe gave him directions.

"South it is."

They traveled in silence until they were out of the city and he was driving along a two-lane highway.

"Do you have an address for the place we're going?"

Phoebe read it to him out of the paper.

"I have no idea where that is." Ryan kept his eyes on the road as a delivery truck whizzed by them.

"It's another half hour down this road, then we have to turn off."

"Have you always redone furniture?" It was ironic that she enjoyed something that was so similar to his passion.

"I've been doing it for a few years. I found I needed to fill the time when Joshua was away."

"You were lonely, weren't you?"

Phoebe didn't immediately answer. "It wasn't so hard at first. But it got more so as time went on."

Her melancholy tone implied that something more than loneliness had pushed her toward finding a hobby.

"Joshua didn't care for my painting taking up my time when he was home so I always put things away then."

He remembered what she'd said before about putting away her painted furniture because Joshua hadn't like it. That had surprised him. It didn't sound like the Joshua he'd known. Maybe he had changed since they'd known each other in the service. Ryan needed to find a safer subject. "Looks like it's going to be a pretty day."

"Yes, it does. I'm glad. I don't want anything I buy to get wet."

"I brought a covering in case we need it."

She gave him a smile of admiration.

The feeling of being a conquering hero went through him. What was happening to him? He smiled back. "Glad I could be of help."

"You're going to need to take a left turn in a couple of miles."

"You know this area well."

"This isn't the first time I've been down this way to garage sales."

They lapsed into silence until Phoebe began giving him directions regularly. They turned off the main road onto a dirt road that led up to a farmhouse with a steep metal roof and a porch circling it on three sides. A large barn with its doors opened wide stood off to the side. Two other cars were parked nearby.

"They keep the stuff they're selling in the barn," Phoebe said, with the door already open.

She hurried to the barn and Ryan joined her halfway there. They entered the dim interior. In an unused stall tables had been set up that contained all types of bottles, kitchen utensils, purses and other small items. On the other side were the larger items. Phoebe headed to them. She studied a cabinet that came up to his chest. It was much too high for her to make good use of it.

Phoebe pulled the drawers out and pushed them back in. "Would you mind tipping it forward so I can look at the back's construction?"

He had to give her credit for being knowledgeable and thorough. Ryan did as she requested.

She knocked against the wood and made a sound in her throat. Her hair curtained her face so he couldn't see what she was thinking. Running a hand over the edge and back again, she made another sound. Whether it was positive or negative he couldn't tell. It didn't matter. He was enthralled just watching her.

"You can let it down now."

Ryan lowered it to the ground.

She stepped back and studied it. "I think it'll do."

"May I make a suggestion?"

She looked at him as if she'd almost forgotten he was there. He didn't like that idea. That he could that easily disappear from her thoughts. Raising her chin and cocking her head, she gave him a questioning look. "Yes?"

"I think this chest is too tall for you. You can't even see over it."

Her eyes widened. She turned to face the chest. "You know, I can't. I hadn't thought about that."

"You need one where you can use all the space. You couldn't even find the baby powder if it got pushed to the back on this one."

"You're right. I guess now that I'm in the baby

mood I'm getting in a panic to buy, afraid that time is running out. That I won't get it all done."

"We have all day. You have more places on your list, don't you?"

"Yes."

"Then let's go see what they have. Maybe we can find just the right one."

He offered his hand.

She looked at it for a moment and then placed hers in his. Her fingers were soft and cool. He closed his around them. It was as if they had chosen to face a problem together and see it overcome. Somehow this relationship had gone from less about getting a piece of furniture to having an emotional attachment. He didn't release her hand when she gave his a nudge.

Together, side by side this time, they walked back to the truck.

They visited two more places and didn't find what Phoebe was looking for.

"I don't know about you but I need something to eat," Ryan said, when he saw a sign for a café and ice-cream parlor.

"I am, too, but we might miss out on my chest."

"Then there'll be another one."

"Okay," Phoebe said, but her heart didn't sound like it was in it.

He pulled into a drive much like the one at the first house they had visited. As he came to the end of it he found a house with a restaurant attached to the back. "Come on. We'll have a sandwich, maybe some ice cream and plan our attack. Bring the paper and the map."

She didn't argue and had them in her hand when he came around the truck to meet her.

Ryan held the door for her to enter the café, then directed her to one of the small square tables in the room. Phoebe took a seat in one of the wooden chairs. He sat beside her.

She looked around the space. "I like this. It's my style."

"It does look like your type of decor."

The tables were covered in floral-print cloths. The chairs were mismatched, like hers.

A young man brought them a menu. He and Phoebe studied it for a moment.

"What're you going to have?" Ryan laid the menu on the table.

"A ham sandwich and lemonade."

"I think I'll have the same."

The waiter returned and Ryan gave him their order. When they were alone again, Ryan said, "Hand me that map, then read out the places you want to visit."

Phoebe did as he asked and he circled the places on the map. "Okay, is that it?"

"Yes."

"All right. Show me on the map your first and second, then third choice."

Phoebe pointed them out. He drew a line from one to the other to the other. "This is our game plan. We'll visit these. If we don't find what you want today, then we'll try again next weekend or whenever we can. Agreed?"

"Agreed."

The waiter brought their meals.

"Now let's eat. I'm starved."

She smiled. "You're always hungry."

Her soft chuckle made his heart catch. He was becoming hungry for more time with her.

Phoebe had always enjoyed junking but never as much as she had today. It turned out that Ryan was not only efficient but also a fun person to have around. She hadn't smiled or laughed as much as she had in the last few weeks. She'd almost forgotten what it was like to have a companion or to just appreciate male company.

Even so, there seemed to be a part of Ryan that he kept to himself. Something locked up that he wouldn't or couldn't share with the world or her.

After they had finished their lunch they climbed back into the truck and headed down the road. This time Ryan was not only driving but navigating as well. It didn't take them long to reach their first stop.

"It looks like they have a lot of furniture," Ryan said as they walked toward a shed.

"Maybe they'll have just the right thing."

A man met them at the shed door but let them wander around and look in peace.

Phoebe had been studying a chest. She turned to speak to Ryan but found he was in another area, looking at a rocker. "What have you found?"

She joined him and watched as he lovingly ran a hand down the arm of the chair. Now that she was closer she could tell it sat lopsided. There was a rocker missing.

"There was a woman who lived next to my foster-family who had a rocker like this. She and only she sat in it. She said it was the best seat in the house."

"She was nice to you."

"Yeah. Her house was where I would go if things got too hard for me at the Henrys'." She could only imagine the little boy who had needed someone on his side. "It's beautiful. I like that high-back style. Gives you someplace to lean your head."

Ryan moved another chair and a small table so that he could pull the rocker out. When he had plenty of space he tipped it over.

Phoebe admired the careful way he took in handling it. Despite his size, he was a gentle man.

"I think I can fix this. The structure is sound. All that's missing is the one rocker. Would you like to have it for the baby's room? I can fix it. You can paint it or I'll stain it."

"You don't need to buy me anything."

He looked at her. "I wasn't buying you anything. I was getting something for the baby."

Before she could argue that it was the same thing, he walked away and had soon agreed a price with the owner.

She didn't find a chest of drawers there but

they left with the rocker tied down in the back of the truck. At the next place she found nothing she liked.

As Ryan drove away she looked out the window. "I don't think we're going to find what I need today."

"Don't give up yet. We still have one more place on our list."

She studied his strong profile for a minute. He had a long jaw that spoke of determination but there were small laugh lines around his eyes. His forehead was high and a lock of hair had fallen across it as if to rebel against control. Much like the man himself.

"Do you always approach everything you do with such determination?"

"I guess old habits die hard. Being in the service will do that to you."

"Tell me what it was like being in the service. Joshua would never talk about it. He always said he didn't want me to worry."

This was the last subject Ryan wished to discuss. He wanted those days long gone and forgotten.

Without his heart in it, he asked, "What do you want to know?"

"Was it as bad as the news makes it out to be?"

"Worse."

"I'm sorry."

"It's war. Few people understand. War is never pretty. It's all death and destruction. Until you have looked into someone's eyes and watched life leave them, no one can ever grasp that."

"That happened to you?"

His glance held disbelief. "Yeah, more than once."

At her gasp he couldn't decide if he was pleased he'd shocked her or disgusted with himself for doing so. "I'm sorry. I shouldn't have said it like that."

"Yes, you should have. You have experienced horrible, unspeakable things while I've been here safe in my home." A second later she asked, "How did you deal with it?"

Ryan gripped the steering wheel and kept his eyes on the road. He wasn't sure he had or was. "I did what I had to and tried not to think about how lives were being shattered."

She laid a hand on his shoulder. Even that small

gesture eased the flames of painful memories. Suddenly he wanted her to understand. "There was this one guy in my unit who had lost half his face. He cried and he kept repeating 'I'm going to scare my kids, I'm going to scare my kids.' How do you reassure someone in that kind of shape that he won't?"

As if a dam had broken he couldn't stop talking. "There was another guy who had tried to kill himself because he'd received a Dear John letter. We were in a war zone and we had our own guys trying to kill themselves."

"That had to be hard to deal with."

"Yeah, more than anyone should have to deal with. We lived in metal shipping containers that had been divided into two small rooms by thin wooden walls. We showered in bath houses, ate in the same mess hall. It's hard not to get involved in each other's lives."

"I imagine you do."

"Even though we had R and R time, you never truly got away from it. We could go to the rec building, call our families or use the internet, but the minute we stepped out of the building the fence and sentries told us we weren't at home."

He'd confessed more than he'd ever told anyone about his time in the service. Had he terrified her? He glanced her direction. A single tear rested on her cheek.

His hand found hers. "I'm sorry. I shouldn't have told you all that."

"I'm glad you did. This baby deserves to know about his daddy and what he did. What life was like for him before he died. Thank you for telling me."

Ryan went back to looking at the road. "Joshua was a strong leader. I saw more than one man panic in the kind of situation we were in in that village. He held it together. Because of him I'm alive and so are a lot of other men. You can tell the baby that his father was a good soldier and a hero."

It was a relief to see the turnoff to their next stop. The conversation had gone in a direction he'd not expected or really wanted to continue. He made the turn into the road leading to the farmhouse. He released Phoebe's hand. The feeling of loss was immediate. "I have a good feeling about this place."

"I hope you're right."

Phoebe's voice held a sad note that he'd like to have disappear. He hadn't intended to bring what had been a nice day to a standstill. Even so, he had to admit it was a relief to get some of what he felt about the war off his chest. He'd carried that heaviness too long. It was strange that Phoebe, the wife of an army buddy, was the one person he had felt comfortable enough with to do so. He had never even told his coworkers as much as he'd just told Phoebe.

The house they were looking for came into view. He pulled to a stop in the drive.

"Doesn't look like we're at the right place. Let me double-check the address." Phoebe opened the newspaper.

A woman came around the corner of the house.

Ryan stepped out of the truck. "Excuse me, ma'am, but is this the place where the yard sale is?" he asked.

"Yes, but it has been over for an hour. We've put everything away."

Phoebe joined them. "Do you still have any furniture? I'm looking for a chest of drawers for my baby's room."

"I'm sorry but we had very little furniture and what we did have is all gone."

Ryan looked at Phoebe. He hated seeing that defeated look on her face. "We'll just have to try again on another weekend."

They were on their way back to the truck when the woman called, "Hey, I do have a chest of drawers out in the old smoke house that my husband says has to go. It was my mother's. It's missing a leg and a drawer, though."

Ryan looked at Phoebe. "I could fix those things. It wouldn't hurt to look."

Phoebe shrugged. "I guess so."

She didn't sound too confident. He gave her an encouraging smile. "Come on. You might be in for a surprise."

He certainly knew about them. Phoebe had been one of those in his life.

"It's back this way." The woman headed around the house. She led them to a wooden building that looked ready to fall down and opened a door.

Ryan looked into the dark space. All types of farming equipment, big and small, was crammed into it.

"You're gonna have to move some of that stuff

around if you want to get to it," the woman said from behind him.

Glancing back over the woman's shoulder to where Phoebe stood, he saw her look of anticipation. Not wanting to disappoint her, he didn't have any choice but to start moving rakes, hoes, carts and even larger gardening implements. He definitely didn't want her to do that.

Picking up things and shifting them aside to make a narrow path, he could see a chest leaning against a wall. In the dim light provided by the slits in the boards it looked the right height. His heart beat faster. It might be just what Phoebe was looking for.

He made his way to it by squeezing between a stack of boxes and a tall piece of farming equipment that he couldn't put a name to. Pulling the chest away from the wall, he leaned it forward to look at the back.

"Doesn't it look perfect? It's just right."

His head jerked toward the voice. "Phoebe! What're you doing back here?" He shouldn't have been surprised. She managed to dumbfound him regularly.

"I wanted to see."

"You should have waited until I brought it out."

"What if you had done all that work and I wasn't interested? I didn't have any problem getting back here, except for between the boxes and that piece of equipment. I'm certainly no larger than you."

He eased the cabinet back against the wall. "What's that supposed to mean?"

"You're no little guy, with your broad shoulders and height."

He wasn't and he liked that she had noticed.

She circled around him, as if wanting to get a closer look at the chest. She pulled each drawer out and examined the slot where the missing drawer went. "What do you think?"

"What?" Ryan was so absorbed with watching her he'd missed her question.

"What do you think?" she asked in an impatient tone. "Can it be fixed?"

"Yes. It has sturdy construction. With a new drawer and a leg you would be in business."

She looked at him and grinned. Had he just been punched in the stomach?

"In business?"

"What kind of business would that be?"

"The baby business," he quipped back.

"I think I'll like that kind of business." Her smile was of pure happiness.

He returned it. "And I think you'll be good at it. So do you want the chest?"

"Yes, I do."

For a second there he wanted her to say that about him. He shook the thought away. Those were not ones he should be having. He and Phoebe were just friends. That was all they could be or should be.

"If you'll slide your way back out, then I'll bring this."

"I could help—"

Ryan leaned down until his nose almost touched hers. "No. You. Will. Not."

She giggled. "I thought that's what you might say." She gave him a quick kiss on the cheek and started for the path. "Thanks. You've been wonderful."

All he could do was stand there with a silly grin on his face. What was he, ten again?

With a groan, he began manipulating the chest through the maze. With less muscle than patience, he managed to get it outside. Before he could hardly stand the cabinet against the side of the building, Phoebe began studying it with a critical eye. She pulled each of the drawers out and pushed them in again.

"What do you want for it?" Phoebe glanced at the lady.

Heck, now that he'd worked to bring it into the light of day it didn't matter what the woman wanted. He'd pay her price just to not have to put it back.

"One hundred dollars," the woman stated.

"It has a leg and a drawer missing. How about thirty?" Phoebe came back with.

"Make it eighty, then."

Ryan watched, his look going from one woman to the other like at a tennis match.

"I don't think so. There's too much work to be done. Thanks anyway." Phoebe started toward the truck.

Ryan stood there in disbelief. She was going to leave after all the looking they had done today and the trouble he'd gone to get the chest out of the cluttered building? After she'd found what she wanted?

He gave her a pointed look. She winked. He was so stunned he couldn't say anything.

"How about we make it fifty?" the woman called after her.

Phoebe made almost a ballerina turn and had a smile on her face when she faced the woman. "Deal." Phoebe opened up her purse and handed the woman some bills.

He had to give Phoebe credit, she was an excellent bargainer.

She looked at him and grinned in pure satisfaction. What would it be like to have her look at him that way because of something he'd done? Heaven.

Clearing his head, he asked, "Ma'am, do you mind if I pull the truck closer to load this up?"

"Sure, that's fine."

Twenty minutes later, Phoebe was waving bye to the woman like they were long-lost friends.

"That was some dickering you did back there."

"Dickering?"

"Bargaining."

"Thanks."

"The next time I have to buy a car I'm taking you with me."

Phoebe smiled.

"Where did you learn to do that?"

"I don't know. I just know that it usually works. And it's always worth a try."

"There for a few minutes I was afraid that I was going to have to wrestle that chest back into that building."

"I wouldn't have let that happen. I wanted it too badly. I would have paid the hundred."

"Well, I'm glad to know that."

A few minutes later he pulled out onto the main highway that would take them to the larger road leading to Melbourne.

"Oh, the little penguins. I haven't seen them since I was young," Phoebe remarked as they passed a billboard.

"Penguins?"

"You don't know about the penguins? At Phillip Island?"

"No."

"They come in every night. It's amazing to watch. They go out every morning and hunt for food and bring it back for their babies. They're about a foot tall."

"How far away is this?"

"On the coast. About thirty minutes from here."

"Do you want to go?"

"They don't come in until the sun is going down. It would be late when we got home."

She sounded so wistful that he didn't have the heart to say no.

"Tell me which way to go."

"Surely you have something to do tonight. A date?"

"Why, Phoebe, are you fishing to find out about my love life?"

She rewarded him with a blush. "No."

"I have no plans. I'd like to see these tuxedo-wearing birds."

"Then you need to turn around and head the other direction."

"Yes, ma'am."

CHAPTER FIVE

PHOEBE HADN'T BEEN to Phillip Island in years. She still had the picture her father had taken of her standing next to the penguin mascot. The area had changed. The building had been expanded and more parking added.

Ryan found a space and pulled into it. "I'm glad we ate when we did. I haven't seen any place to do so in miles."

"I was hungry, too."

Inside the welcome center they were directed outside. In another hour it would be dark. They followed the paved path that zigged and zagged down toward the beach. Other people mingled along the way.

"What's that noise?" Ryan asked.

"That's the baby chicks."

He looked around. "Where are they?"

Phoebe placed a hand on his arm. She pointed with the other at a hole in the grass embankment.

"They're in there. Watch for a second and you'll catch a glimpse of them."

A grin came to Ryan's lips. "I see one."

"The penguin's mother and father leave the nest in the morning and spend all day hunting food. They return each night to feed the young and do it all over again the next day. Fifty kilometers or farther."

"Every day?" Ryan asked in an incredulous tone.

"Yes. The ocean is overfished so they have to go farther and farther. It's pretty amazing what parents will do for their children."

Ryan looked at her. "Are you scared?"

"Some. At first I was shocked, frightened, mad, then protective. It has been better here lately." She left off *because of you.*

"So it takes both parents to find enough food?"

"They are partners for life."

Ryan looked off toward the ocean and didn't say anything.

Had she made him nervous? Made it sound like she expected something from him? "I think I'm most scared that I won't be enough for the baby. That I can't be both mother and father."

"I think you'll do just fine. Your baby will grow up happy and loved. Let's head on down."

Phoebe didn't immediately move. Did he think she expected him to offer to help? That she thought he'd be around when the baby came? Would take Joshua's place? She wouldn't force commitment on any man. She was looking for someone who wanted to spend time with her. Who would put her first, over everything. Someone that would willingly be there for her and her baby.

She started walking but at a slower pace.

They walked in silence around a couple of turns before Ryan said, "Whew, the smell is something."

"There are thousands of small chicks living in this bank."

"Really?" Ryan leaned over the rail and peered down. "I don't see them."

"Most are asleep right now. When they wake up you can see their heads stick out. There is one small nest after another."

"Everywhere."

Phoebe chuckled. It was fun to be around when Ryan experienced something new. He seemed to get such enjoyment and wonderment from it. It made her see it the same way. "Yes, they are everywhere."

"If you had told me about this I wouldn't have believed it."

"You haven't seen the best yet. Come on, let's get a good seat."

"Seat for what?"

"To watch mum and dad come home." She took his hand and pulled him along the walk.

When she tried to let his hand go he hung on tighter. She relaxed and reveled in the feeling of having someone close. Ryan seemed to like having contact with her.

"What do you mean?"

"We have to go down to the beach. There are grandstands."

"Like bleachers?"

"Come on, I'll show you."

As they continued on Ryan pulled her to a halt every once in a while to peer into the bank. "I can't believe all these little birds here."

She just smiled. They finally made it down to the sand. She was glad to have Ryan's help as she crossed it and they found a seat on an aluminum bench.

Ryan looked around. "This many people will be here?"

"Yes, the three sets of bleachers will be full and there will be people standing along the rails."

"I wonder why I've never heard about this."

"I don't know but I do think it's the best-kept secret about Australia."

The bleachers filled as the sun began to set. Minutes later the crowd around them quieted.

"Look," Phoebe whispered and pointed out toward the water. "Here they come."

Emerging from the surf was a small penguin, and behind it another until there was a group of ten to twelve. They hurried up the beach and into the grassy areas.

A loud chirping rose as their chicks realized dinner had arrived. Soon after the first group, another one came out of the water. Then another. Occasionally the group would be as many as twenty.

Ryan leaned close. There was a smell to him that was all Ryan with a hint of the sea. Phoebe liked the combination.

"Why do they come out in groups?"

"For protection from predators. If they all come at once, then they all could be killed. They come out in groups and in waves. That way there will be someone left to take care of the chicks if something happens to them."

Who would take care of her child if something happened to her? She wasn't going to think about that. Glancing at Ryan, she saw that he was looking out at the water. Was he thinking about what she'd said?

As they watched the penguins, the sun went down and floodlights came on. Phoebe shivered as a breeze came off the water. Ryan put an arm around her and pulled her in close. She didn't resist his warmth. Instead, she snuggled into his side.

As they watched, a cluster came out of the water and quickly returned.

"See, that group was frightened by something. Watch for a minute and they will try it again."

Out of the water they came. Ryan gave her a little squeeze.

"You know, I expected the penguins to have black coats but they are really a dark navy."

"That was my biggest surprise the first time I saw them. Aren't they cute?"

"I have to admit they are."

They watched for the next hour. As they did so the penguins continued to come out in waves and the noise from the nests rose to almost a point to where Ryan and Phoebe couldn't hear each other.

Finally they sat there for another ten minutes and no more birds arrived. The crowd started moving toward the walkway.

"Is that it?" Ryan sounded disappointed.

"That's it for tonight."

"Amazing."

When they passed a park ranger, Ryan asked, "How many penguins are there?"

"Two thousand two hundred and fifty-one tonight."

"How do you know that?"

"We count them. There are rangers stationed in sections along the beach."

Ryan's arm supported her as they climbed the hill on the way back to the welcome center. He didn't remove it as they walked to the truck.

As they left the car park he said, "Thanks for bringing me. I'll be doing this again."

"I'm glad you had a good time."

"I did. I bet you are beat." He grinned. "You didn't even fall asleep on me today."

"I'm sorry. I can't help it."

"I'm just teasing you."

They talked about their day for a few minutes. It was the best one she'd had in a long time. Even before Joshua had died. Ryan had proved he could be fun and willing to try new things. She had more than enjoyed his company. Unfortunately, she feared she might crave it. Her eyelids became heavy and a strong arm pulled her against a firm cushion.

Ryan hated to wake Phoebe but they were in front of her house. He had given thought to just sitting in the truck and holding her all night.

Visiting the penguins had been wonderful. He'd especially enjoyed the look on Phoebe's face when the first bird had waddled out of the water. It was pure pleasure. He'd like the chance to put a look on her face like that.

That was a place he shouldn't go. He'd been more than uncomfortable when the discussion had turned to how parents protected their young.

He couldn't be that person in Phoebe's life and the baby's. That devotion those tiny birds had to their young wasn't in him. He couldn't let Phoebe start believing that it was. He wouldn't be around for the long haul. That required a level of emotion that he wasn't willing to give.

Still, she felt right in his arms. Too right.

He pushed those thoughts away and settled for practicality and what was best for Phoebe. She would be sore from sleeping in the truck and he would ache for other reasons. He smirked. Plus he was liable to end up in jail when her neighbor called the police.

"Phoebe." He shook her gently. "Phoebe. We're home."

Her eyes fluttered open. "Mmm…?"

"We're at your house."

"Oh." She tried to sit up but it wasn't happening quickly.

"I'm sorry, I didn't mean to fall asleep on you, literally and figuratively."

"Not a problem." And it hadn't been.

Ryan opened his door and got out before helping her out. He walked her to the door.

"What about my chest of drawers?"

"I need to fix the leg and build a drawer before you can do much with it anyway. I'll just take it home with me. You could come to my house and work on it. I'll do the paint stripping anyway. You don't need to be around those fumes."

"You've already done so much."

Ryan put a hand under her chin and lifted it. "Hey, today was no hardship for me."

She smiled. "I enjoyed it, too."

With reluctance he stepped back. "You need to get to bed."

"And you still have a drive ahead."

"I do. I'll see you in clinic Wednesday afternoon. Plan to come to my place afterward. I should have the leg on and the drawer done by then."

"Okay."

He liked the fact that she readily agreed.

"See you then."

Phoebe made her way into the hospital and up to the clinic waiting room. She hadn't been this nervous since her first visit. Her name was called and she was directed to an examination room. She was told to remove her trousers, sit on the exam table and place the sheet over her. Soon Sophia entered. "Well, have you made a decision on who you want to replace me?"

"Not yet. I hate to lose you. Are you sure you can't put off the wedding until after this baby is born?"

"I don't think Aiden will agree to that. You're going to have to make a decision soon."

"I know."

"I'm sorry that I can't be there to deliver." Sophia's smile grew. "But love doesn't wait."

"I understand. I wish you the best."

"So how's it going between you and Ryan? I know your first meeting was a little rocky."

Phoebe smiled. "That would be an understatement. It turns out he's a great guy. He's been helping me get the baby's room together. I asked him to put the baby bed together and he volunteered to paint the room."

"I'm not surprised. He's the kind of person who keeps to himself and quietly goes about helping people."

A few minutes later Sophia had left and Phoebe had just finished dressing when there was a knock on the door. "Come in."

Ryan entered. "Hey."

"Hi." She sounded shy even to herself. She'd never been timid in her life.

"So how're you feeling?"

"Fine."

"Great. No aches or pains after our adventure on Saturday?"

She appreciated his friendly manner. "I was tired but no more than I'm sure you were."

"I have to admit it was a long day. You mind waiting on me in the waiting room? I have one more patient to see."

"Sure."

She hadn't been waiting long when he came out of the office area.

"You ready?"

She stood. "Ryan, I have to work tomorrow. I can't be out late. Maybe I should just come by this weekend."

"Don't you want to see what I've done with the chest?"

Ryan sounded like a kid wanting to show off his new toy. He opened the door leading to the main hall. She went out and he followed.

"Sure I do, but I also have to get to bed at a decent hour."

"I'll drive you home."

"I don't want you to have to do that."

He looked at her. Worry darkened his eyes to a granite color. "Is something wrong? Did I do something wrong?"

"No, of course not."

"Then stop arguing and come on. I'll get you home for your regular bedtime. We'll go to my place and then walk down to a café for dinner. Then I'll take you home."

"Okay. If you insist."

"I do."

Twenty minutes later Ryan unlocked the front door to his home. She followed him in. The place looked no different than it had the last time she had been there yet everything had changed. She felt welcomed where she hadn't before.

Ryan dropped his clothes in a pile next to the door just as he had done before. "Are you thirsty?" he called from the kitchen area.

"No, but I would like to use the bathroom."

"That's right. Pregnant women and their bladders. You'll find it off my bedroom. Sorry it isn't cleaner."

"I'll try not to look."

Phoebe walked to the only doorway she'd never been through. She stopped in shock. The most perfect bedroom suite she'd ever seen filled the room. The furnishing here was nothing like what was in the rest of the house. There was such a contrast it was like being in two different worlds. She went to the sleigh-style bed and ran her hand along the footboard, then turned to study the large dresser. The workmanship was old world with a twist of the modern. She'd never seen any like it. She'd give anything to have furniture like this.

"Hey, Phoebe—" Ryan walked into the room.

"These are beautiful pieces. Where did you get them?" She walked around the end of the bed to the bedside table. She couldn't stop herself from touching it.

"I made it."

She pivoted. "You did? It's amazing. If you ever give up being a midwife, you could become a millionaire, making furniture. It's just beautiful."

A hint of redness crept up his throat.

"Thank you. I don't think it's that good. But I'm glad you like it. You ready to go downstairs?"

"Downstairs?"

"That's where my workshop is."

"I haven't made it to the bathroom yet."

"You go. The door to the basement is in the kitchen. I'll leave it open."

A few minutes later Phoebe gingerly descended the stairs. She was half way down when Ryan rushed over.

"Give me your hand and I'll help you. I forget how steep the steps are."

"I think I've got it." She took the last three steps, then looked around. The area was immaculate. There was equipment spaced around the room that she couldn't put a name to but there wasn't a speck of sawdust on the floor. It was in marked contrast to his living area upstairs. He obviously loved and spent a lot of time down here.

Her cabinet stood near a wooden workbench. Ryan walked over to it. There was a look of anticipation on his face. As if it really mattered to him what she thought. He moved from one foot to the other. The man was worried about her re-action.

"So what do you think?"

"About what?"

"The chest."

"I know what you're talking about, silly. I'm just teasing you. It looks wonderful."

As if he'd been awarded a prize, his chest puffed out. She would have never thought that this self-assured man would be that concerned about her opinion.

"I couldn't find a leg that matched the others so I bought four new ones that were as close to the original as I could find."

"They look great. The drawer looks like it was made with it. I'm not surprised after I saw your bedroom furniture. Thank you, Ryan. It's per-fect."

"I managed to strip some of the paint but it still needs more work. I was going to do some of it tonight but I promised to get you home."

"You know I'd rather have that finished so I can work on it than go out for a meal. Why don't I go down to the café and get takeout—?"

"While I work?" Ryan finished with a grin. "I think you could be a slave driver for a little bit."

"You're the one that said I shouldn't be stripping it. I would have put it out in the backyard where there was plenty of ventilation."

He propped his hands on his hips. "And just how were you planning to move it out of the weather?"

"I would have found a way. Ms. Rosenheim could help me."

"That would have been a sight worth watching."

She glared at him. "You don't think we could do it?"

He threw up his hands. "I don't think I would put anything past you two."

"Good. You need to remember that. Now, I'm going to get us something to eat and you'd better get busy."

"Yes, ma'am."

His chuckle followed her up the stairs.

Ryan was aware of Phoebe returning. Her soft footfalls crossed overhead. As she moved around in the kitchen, something about the sound made him feel good inside. When her eyes lit up at the sight of the chest of drawers he felt like he could carry the world on his shoulders. For so long he'd only seen the look in eyes of those in pain or life slipping away. He could do nothing to change it but this time he'd been able to help someone and see pure joy. It was the same feeling he had when he delivered a baby.

Taking the can of paint stripper off the bench, he poured it into an empty food can. Using a brush, he applied it to the wood of the chest.

He liked too many things about Phoebe. The way her hair hid her face like a curtain and then when it was drawn away discovering she'd hidden a smile from him. The way she insisted on helping. Phoebe was no shrinking violet. She was a survivor. JT's baby was lucky. JT's baby!

What was happening to him? Phoebe was JT's wife. *Was.* It didn't matter how attracted to her he was, she would always belong to JT. There was the bro code. You don't take your best friend's girl.

Ryan picked up the putty knife and began to scrape the paint off in thin sheets.

No matter how much you might want to.

A board creaked above him.

It didn't matter. Phoebe didn't feel that way about him. She'd been alone during a hard time in her life and she was searching for a connection to JT. All *he* meant to her was someone who had known the father of her baby. He would be her friend and nothing more.

Still, it was as if he saw the world as a better place when he was around her. Like his wounds were finally closing. That life could be good. Not black-and-white. Living or dying. But happy, healthy and hopeful.

"Hey, down there, your dinner is served." There was a cheerful tone to her voice, like someone calling another they cared about.

Ryan's heart thumped hard against his chest. Wouldn't it be nice to be called to every meal that way? Even those little things improved life.

Phoebe was filling their glasses when Ryan's footsteps drew her attention to the door of the basement. It had been over a year since she had called someone to dinner and here she was doing it twice in less than two weeks. She liked it. There was something about it that made her feel like all was as it should be in her world.

"Smells good."

"You do know that all I did was pick it up, don't you?" she said, putting the pitcher back on the corner.

"Yes, but you did a good job with that."

He looked at the table. She had set their places with what little she could find in Ryan's woefully low-stocked kitchen. Passing a shop, she'd impulsively bought a handful of flowers. She hoped he didn't think she was suggesting that this was more than a friendly meal.

He nodded toward them. "Nice touch."

She smiled. "I like fresh flowers. I couldn't resist them."

"I'll have to remember that. Let me wash my hands."

Ryan went to the sink. With his back to her she had a chance for a good look. What would it be like to run her hands across these wide shoulders? To cup what must be a firm butt?

She didn't need to be thinking like that. But she was pregnant, not dead.

"What's wrong? You feeling okay? You have an odd look on your face."

She'd been caught ogling him. "No, no, I feel fine."

A slow smile stole over his face and his eyes twinkled, pushing the worry away. "Okay, let's eat. I'm hungry."

Had he figured out what she'd been thinking?

They each took one of the two chairs at the table.

"I didn't know what you liked so I got two kinds of soups and two sandwiches, hoping you liked at least one of each."

"It all looks good."

"I didn't move your mail off the table. I thought you might not be able to find it if I did." She pushed it toward him. Ryan's hand brushed hers when he reached for it.

The flutter in her middle had nothing to do with the baby moving. She jerked her hand back.

"Is that a valid comment on my housekeeping skills?"

"Not really, but now that you mention it I've not really seen any of those skills outside your shop."

He laughed. "I deserve that. I'm not here much

and when I am I go downstairs. As for my mail, I usually let it stack up and then open anything that isn't bills when I get around to it." He glanced through the pile and pulled an envelope out, tearing it open. Slipping a card out, he studied it a moment, then laid it on the table. "It's an invitation to Sophia's wedding next weekend."

"You weren't kidding. That had to have come weeks ago."

He gave her a sheepish look. "I'm sure it did."

"I'm happy for her but I hate it she isn't going to be there to deliver this baby. I've become attached to her. It's hard to give her up. I don't want just anyone to deliver. But I've got to make a choice soon."

There was a long pause before Ryan leaned forward and said, "I'd like to do it."

Phoebe sucked in a breath. "You want to do what?"

"Be your midwife. Would you let me take over from Sophia?"

She wasn't sure it was a good idea but she didn't want to hurt his feelings by saying no immediately. She'd been looking for emotional support, not medical help. Ryan being her midwife sounded far too personal. "Ooh, I don't know if I'm comfortable with that."

"You need a midwife and I'm one."

"Yes, but isn't there something about not delivering people you know?"

His gaze held hers. "I don't see it as being a problem. And I'd rather be the one there if there's a complication than wishing I had been."

She nodded.

"Phoebe, I'd like to be a part of bringing Joshua's baby into the world."

Wasn't this what she'd been looking for? Someone to support her? Be there for her? She loved Sophia but she wasn't available. Why shouldn't Ryan be the one? Because she had feelings for him that had nothing to do with the baby.

He shifted forward in his chair. "I didn't mean to put you on the spot."

"No, no. It's okay. I'm just not sure what to say. Let me think about it."

"Take all the time you need."

She didn't have much time. He had proved more than once he was the guy Joshua had said he was. What she knew was that she didn't feel as alone as she had only a few weeks ago. Ryan had been tender and caring with her so why wouldn't he be a good midwife? Right now what she needed to do was change the subject. "Where's Sophia getting married?"

"I forget women are always interested in a wedding." He slid the card toward her.

Phoebe picked it up. It was a classic embossed invitation. "They're getting married at Overnewton. It'll be a beautiful wedding. That's an amazing place."

Ryan gazed at her over his soup spoon.

"What wedding doesn't a woman think is beautiful?"

"Mine wasn't. We got married at the registry office."

"Oh?"

"It was time for Joshua to ship out and we decided to just do it. I wore my best dress and he his dress uniform. And we did it."

"Do you wish you'd had a fancier wedding?"

"Sometimes. But that was us back then. Fast in love, fast to the altar. It seemed exciting. My parents were gone. My brother showed up and one of Joshua's friends from school was there.

We all went out to eat lunch afterward. The next day Joshua was gone."

"No honeymoon?"

"We took a trip into the mountains, camping, when he came home nine months later. Those were good times."

It was nice to talk about Joshua. People were hesitant to ask about him. They were always afraid it would make her cry. What they didn't understand was that she wanted to talk about the husband she'd lost. Wanted to remember. She and Joshua had had some fun times. It was a shame they had grown apart there at the end. She'd wanted better for him. For him to think of her positively.

She picked up her sandwich. "How about you? Ever been married?"

"No."

"Not even close?"

"Nope. Never found the right one."

"I bet there have been women who thought you were the right one."

He shrugged.

"So you've been a 'love them and leave them' guy?"

Ryan looked at her. "I wouldn't say that. It's more like it's better not to get involved unless your heart is fully in it. Mine never has been."

His eyes held a dark look, despite the effortlessness of the words. There was more to it than that but she didn't know him well enough to probe further. "I guess that's fair."

"You know, Joshua used to talk about you all the time. It was Phoebe this and Phoebe that."

"Really?" She'd always thought she'd been more like a toy that he'd come home to play with and then left behind to pick up again during the next holiday. Would things have been different between them if Joshua had not been gone so much?

"He talked about how you liked to camp and hike. What a good sport you were. I liked to hear stories about places you went, things you did."

Guilt washed through her. And the last time Joshua had been home they'd done nothing special. Instead, they'd talked about getting a divorce. How had their relationship deteriorated so much? Would anyone ever love her like she needed to be loved? Want to come home to her every night? Have a family? She put down her half-eaten sandwich and pushed back her chair. "I need to get this cleaned up and get home. It's getting late."

"Do you mind if I finish my sandwich before we go?"

"I'm sorry. I didn't mean to be rude." She settled in her chair again.

"It's okay."

Phoebe watched as Ryan finished his meal. As soon as he had she started removing their plates and glasses.

"I need to put a cover over a few things before we leave." Ryan went down the stairs.

Ten minutes later she called through the door to the basement, "I'm ready to go when you are."

"I'll be right up."

Coming from Ryan, she could depend on it happening.

CHAPTER SIX

JUST UNDER AN hour later Ryan joined Phoebe on the sidewalk in front of her house.

"Thanks for the ride home."

"When are you planning to come to my house and work on the cabinet? This weekend? I'll have it ready for you by then."

"I hadn't thought about that. I guess I need to get busy. I'll bring my paints and be there early on Saturday morning."

"I can come get you—"

"No, I'll take the tram." She started up the walk.

"I don't mind."

She looked at him. "Ryan, please."

"Okay, okay. Have it your way. Come on, you're tired." He took her elbow and they started toward the door.

Phoebe stopped walking.

Ryan jerked to a stop. "What—?"

She kicked off her shoes and picked them up by two fingers. "My feet are killing me."

They continued to the door. Phoebe unlocked it, pushing it open.

"If you soak and massage your feet it would help," Ryan said behind her.

"I don't do feet." She dropped her shoes inside the door.

Ryan followed her in and closed the door behind him. "That's all right, because I do. You get a bath and come back here. Bring a bottle of your favorite lotion with you. I'll be waiting."

"It's late. We've both had a long day."

"It won't take long and I promise you'll like it. So stop complaining and go on."

Phoebe gave him a dubious look but went off toward her bedroom.

While she was gone Ryan found a cook pot and put water on to heat. Looking under the sink, he pulled out a wash pan. He added a little dish soap to it. He searched the cabinets for a container of salt and, finding it, he added a generous amount to the soap. When the water started to steam he poured it into the pan.

Going to the bathroom in the hallway, he pulled

a towel off the rack. Returning to the living room, he placed the towel on the floor in front of the most comfortable-looking chair. He then went for the pan of water.

"What's all this?" Phoebe asked. She wore a gown and a housecoat that covered her breasts but not her belly. Her hair flowed around her shoulders and her cheeks were rosy. Ryan had never seen a more captivating sight.

Gathering his wits and settling his male libido, he took her hand and led her toward the chair. "I'm going to help make those feet feel better. You sit here."

She lowered herself into the chair.

"Now, slowly put your feet into the water. It may be too hot."

"This feels wonderful." She sighed, lowering her feet into the water.

He left her to get a chair from the kitchen, returned and placed it in front of her.

"What're you planning now?"

Taking a seat, he faced her. "I'm going to massage your feet."

"I'm not letting you do that!"

"Why not? You ticklish?"

Phoebe didn't look at him. "No."

"I think you're lying to me. Did you bring the lotion?"

She shifted to her right and put her hand in her housecoat pocket. She pulled out a bottle and handed it to him. Without even opening the bottle he recognized the scent he thought of as hers. He reached down, his hand wrapping her calf and lifting it to rest on his thigh.

"I'm getting you wet." She tried to pull her foot away.

He held it in place. "If it isn't bothering me, then don't let it bother you. Lean back and relax. Close your eyes."

He squirted a liberal amount of lotion into his palm and began rubbing Phoebe's foot. At the first touch she flinched and her eyes popped open. Their gazes met as he began to massage her skin. Seconds later, her eyes closed and she relaxed. As he worked the tissue on the bottom of her foot she let out a soft moan.

"Where did you learn this?" she asked almost with a sigh.

"In the army. The men in the hospital always

seemed to respond and became calmer if they had a massage of some kind."

"I can understand that."

His hands moved to her ankle and then along her calf, kneading the muscles.

"I'm sorry if I put you in a difficult position when I asked to be your midwife." He squeezed more lotion into his hand and started at her toes again and pushed upward.

"It was sweet of you to ask."

He wasn't sure that Phoebe thinking of him as sweet was to his liking.

"Well, something that was said seemed to upset you." He gently pulled on one of her toes.

"It wasn't what you said as much as something I remembered."

"I guess it wasn't a good one." His fingers continued to work her toes.

"No. When Joshua was home the last time, we talked about separating."

"That's tough." He moved up to her knee and started down again.

"We had grown apart. I had my life and he had his. We just didn't make sense anymore." A tone of pain surrounded every word.

"I'm sorry to hear that. It must really have been difficult to deal with when you realized you were pregnant."

"That would be an understatement. How about an ocean of guilt?"

Ryan could more than understand that feeling. He placed her foot back into the pan and picked up the other one. He gave the second one the same attention as he had the first.

Phoebe leaned back and neither one of them spoke for the next few minutes. Ryan was content to watch the expression of pleasure on her face.

"You sure know the way to a woman's heart."

His hands faltered on her calf. He didn't want her heart. Having someone's heart meant they expected some emotion in return. He didn't get that involved with anyone.

Her eyes opened and met his look. There was a realization in them of what she'd said. Regardless of what his mind told him, his body recognized and reacted to the longing in her eyes. His hands moved to massage her knee and above, just as he had done before, but this time the movements requested more. Unable to resist, his fingers brushed the tender tissue of her inner thigh.

* * *

Phoebe was no longer thinking about her feet. This gorgeous, intelligent hunk of man in front of her wanted her. She couldn't remember the last time she'd felt desired. If it had ever felt this compelling.

Ryan's gaze captured hers. His eyes were storm-cloud gray. He held her leg with one hand and slowly trailed a finger upward past her knee to tease her thigh again before bring it down. It was no longer a massaging motion but a caress. With what looked like regret in his eyes, he lowered her foot into the water.

With his gaze still fixed on her, he offered both of his hands.

She took them. He gently pulled her closer and closer until she was in an upright position. Leaning forward, his mouth drew near. "I may be making a huge mistake but I can't help myself."

Ryan's lips were firm, full and sure as they rested on hers. He pressed deeper.

Phoebe wanted more but wasn't sure what that was or if she should want it. This was the first kiss she'd had since Joshua's parting one. She pulled away, their lips losing contact. Her eyes lifted and her look met Ryan's. He didn't hold it. Without a word, he scooped her up into his arms. She wrapped her hands around his neck.

"What?"

"Just be quiet." The words were a low growl. He carried her down the hall to her bedroom and stood her on her feet next to her bed. "Get in."

His tone was gruff. She didn't question, instead doing as he asked. He tucked the extra pillow under her middle and pulled the covers over her shoulders before he turned off the light and left the room. "Good night, Phoebe."

Had he been as affected by the kiss as she had? She still trembled inside. Ryan's lips meeting hers had been wonderful and shocking at the same time. He had surprised her. Everything had remained on a friendly level until his hand had moved up her leg. She'd wanted his kiss but hadn't been sure what to do when she'd got it.

Those days of schoolgirl insecurity had returned. She was soon going to be a mother. Did he feel sorry for her because of the baby? Joshua? Or just because he thought she needed the attention at the moment? The doubts had made her pull away. Now she regretted doing so. Her body longed for him. But it couldn't be. She wouldn't have Ryan feel obligated to her because of her situation. She'd put him on the spot when she'd shown up at his house and she had no intention of doing that to him again. It was best for them just to remain friends.

A few minutes later the front door was opened and closed. Ryan had gone. She didn't have to wonder if the pan and chair had been put away or the front door secured. Ryan would have taken care of that just like she knew she could rely on him to be there for her.

Ryan couldn't sleep and any time he couldn't do that he went to his workshop. What had he been thinking when he'd kissed Phoebe? That was the problem. He hadn't been thinking but feeling. Something he couldn't remember doing in a long time. The need to do more than touch her had pulled at him to the point he'd been unable to stand it any longer. When she'd raised those large questioning eyes…

How could he have done it? He had kissed his dead best friend's wife. Someone who had trusted him. Could there be a greater betrayal?

He'd stepped over the line. Way over. Both personally and professionally. It wouldn't happen again. He could put his personal feelings aside and concentrate on the professional. That was enough of those thoughts.

He had the chest of drawers to finish and sand, and there was also the rocking chair to repair. Phoebe would be here in two days ready to work on them. Soon that baby's room would be complete and the baby here. Then he could back out of Phoebe's life. He would have done then what he could do to honor JT. Phoebe would no longer need him.

Had he seen a cradle at Phoebe's? She would need a cradle for the first few months to keep the newborn close. He'd been given some pink silkwood by an associate who was moving out of town. It had been stored away for a special project. This was it.

Would he have time to get it done before the baby came? If he worked on it every chance he had, he might make it. He'd finish the chest and then start on the cradle. If he worked on the rocker while Phoebe was busy painting, he could keep the cradle a surprise.

He had plenty to do so there wouldn't be time to think about Phoebe. The feel of her lips. The desire in her eyes. The need that was growing in him. With his mind and hands busy he wouldn't be tempted to kiss her again. He had to get control of his emotions. In Iraq he'd been the king of control. He needed to summon some of that now. Compartmentalize when he was around Phoebe. Keep that door she was pushing open firmly closed.

On Saturday morning Ryan came home as the sun was coming up. He'd been gone all night, delivering a baby. Phoebe would be there in a few hours. He wanted to get some sleep before she arrived. Taking a quick bath, he crawled into bed.

He woke with a start. Something wasn't right. The room was too bright. He groaned. He'd slept longer than he'd planned. But something else was off.

Music. His workshop. He had a radio there. Had he left it on?

Wearing only his boxer shorts, he headed for the kitchen. The music grew louder. The basement door stood wide open and a humming mixed with the song playing drifted up the stairs.

He moved slowly down the steps, being careful not to make a noise. Halfway down, he bent over to see who was there.

Phoebe. She sat on a stool with her back to him, painting a side of the chest. She'd been smart enough to open the outside door to let out any fumes. Ryan trod on the next step hard enough that she would hear it. He didn't want to scare her by calling her name.

She twisted around. "Hey."

There was a tentative sound to her voice. Was she thinking about what had happened the last time they had seen each other? Was she worried he might try to kiss her again? He needed to put her at ease. "Hey, yourself. You're not afraid of being hurt when you come into someone's house while they're sleeping?"

"I knocked and knocked. I tried the front door and it was open. I came in and saw you were sleeping. I figured you'd had a late night and had left it open for me."

He nodded. Some of that was true, except he had planned to be up when she arrived. "I had a delivery early this morning."

"How's the mother and baby?"

He moved down the stairs going to stand beside her. "Great. Beautiful girl named Margaret."

"Nice. What do you think?" She indicated the work she'd been doing.

Phoebe had left the wood a natural color and was painting a vine with flowers down the side. "Looks great. What're your plans for the rest of it?"

"I'm going to paint the drawers different colors and paint the other side like this one."

"Sounds nice. Well, I'm going up and see if I can find some breakfast. Then I'll be back down."

He was headed up the stairs when Phoebe said in a bright voice, "Hey, Ryan. I like those boxers. Very sexy."

There was the straightforward Phoebe he'd come to appreciate. Ryan glanced down and shook his head. He'd forgotten all about what he was wearing. "Thanks. I do try."

Phoebe laughed. Ryan did have a good sense of humor. She liked that about him. In fact, she liked too much. He was sexy man and a good kisser, as well. He hadn't mention the kiss or even acted as if he would try again. She couldn't let that happen. Her life was already too complicated. She wouldn't add another emotional turn to it. If he didn't say something, she would have to.

A harsh word filled the air.

She heaved herself off the stool and walked to the door. Another harsh word and pounding on the floor filled the air. She climbed the stairs.

Ryan stood at the sink with the water running.

She moved to his side. "What happened?"

"I burned my finger."

Phoebe smirked at his whiny tone. She went to the refrigerator and opened the freezer compartment. Taking out an ice cube, she handed it to him. "Here, hold this over it."

With a chagrined twist to his mouth he took it. Phoebe looked around the kitchen, found a napkin from a fast-food restaurant and handed that to him, as well. He placed the ice in it and put it on his finger.

"Nothing like the big strong medic needing a medic."

"Hey, taking care of someone hurt is different than being hurt yourself."

She grinned. "Or cooking. Looks like you were having eggs and bacon."

Phoebe pulled the pan that looked as if it had been hastily pushed to the back burner forward and turned on the stove. The bacon was half-cooked.

"I didn't mean for you to come up and cook for me. I'm interrupting your painting."

"It can wait."

She picked up the two eggs sitting on the counter. Cracking them, she let them drop into the pan. There was a *ding*. The toast popped up.

Ryan pulled the slices out and placed them on a plate. "See, I can make toast without hurting myself."

"You get a gold star for that."

"Is that what you give your students when they're good?"

"Fifth years are too old for that sort of thing. Mostly they are happy to get to be first in line to lunch."

He stood nearer than she was comfortable with, but there was nowhere for her to go and still see what she was cooking. It made her body hum just to have him close. This was not what she'd told herself should happen.

"JT was very proud of the fact you're a teacher."

"Really? I always felt like he resented me having to go to work when he was home." Phoebe lifted the bacon, then the two fried eggs out of the pan, placing them beside the toast. She put the frying pan on the back burner and turned off the stove.

Ryan took the plate and sat down at the table. "Maybe that was because he wanted to spend as much normal time with you as possible. Nothing was normal where we were. People thought differently, ate differently, dressed differently. Everything was different. When I had leave I just wanted as much normalcy as I could get."

She slid into the chair across from him. "Then why did he always look forward to going back?"

"I don't know if I can really answer that question. Because it was his job. Because you feel like you're doing something bigger than yourself, something important. You're helping people who can't help themselves. Then there's the excitement. The adrenaline rush can be addictive.

"What I do know is that JT was good at his job. He was good to his men, protected them at any cost, even to himself."

She nodded. Some of the ache over their last words left her. "Thanks for telling me. Now I better understand why he always seemed so eager to return. Sometimes I worried it was more to get away from me. If you think you can finish up your breakfast without injuring yourself, I'll go and work on the chest."

Half an hour later Ryan went down the stairs. "I'm just going to work over here, out of your way."

"You're not going to be in my way."

Over the next hour they said little to each other as they both concentrated on their own projects. Every once in a while she glanced at Ryan. It appeared as if he was drawing off a pattern onto a plank of wood once when she looked. Another time he looked like he was studying a pattern he had spread across the workbench. There was something easy and comfortable about the two of them doing their own things together. It was the companionship she had been missing in her marriage.

Phoebe rubbed her hand over the baby as she looked at the painting she'd just completed. The world would be a good place for him or her. She felt more confident about that now. Glancing at Ryan, she found him with his butt leaning against the bench looking at her.

"Is something wrong?"

"No, I was just enjoying watching you."

Warmth flooded her. She had to stop this now or their new-found friendship might be damaged. She needed it too much to let that happen. "Uh, Ryan, about the other night…"

Ryan tensed slightly, as if he was unsure what she was going to say next.

"Why did you kiss me?"

"Because I wanted to." His eyes never wavered. Ryan was being just as direct.

She shifted on the stool. "That's nice but it can't happen again."

"Why not? We're both adults. I'm attracted to you. I believe you like me. So why not?"

"Because I don't think I can handle any more emotional baggage right now. I've lost a husband who died thinking I no longer loved him. Finding out I was expecting his baby was a shock of a lifetime. Realizing I'm going to have to raise a baby on my own is all I can handle right now. I can't take on more upheaval. I just think it would be easier if we remain friends and friends only."

He nodded. "I understand." Then he turned back to his work at the bench.

Phoebe believed he did. But she hadn't missed that he'd made no promises. She pressed her lips together. Did she really want him to?

Ryan opened the door to the examination room at the clinic the next Wednesday afternoon. To his shock, Phoebe was his next patient. He hadn't seen her since Saturday around noon when he'd had to leave her to deliver a baby. He'd told her she could stay as long as she wished and just to close up before she left as he doubted he'd be home before she was ready to leave.

Hours later he'd arrived home to a neat and tidy house. His bed had been made and his kitchen spotless. Even his pile of dirty clothes had gone. They were neatly folded on his bed. He'd had to admit it was nice to be cared for. It would be easy to get used to.

He'd been astonished at how much he'd missed Phoebe in the next few days and how much he was looking forward to seeing her again. After her statement about nothing more happening between them he didn't want to push her further away. Still, the thought of kissing her kept running through his mind. He'd be tempted when he saw her, but instead he would put on his professional hat and control himself.

"Hi, Phoebe," he said, as he stepped into the room and to the end of the table she was sitting on so he could face her. "This is a surprise."

She smiled. "Hey."

"Thanks for cleaning my house. You shouldn't have but I'm glad you did."

"It was nothing. It gave me something to do while I waited for the paint to dry. I saw the rocker. It looks great. You have a real talent."

"Thanks. Did you ask to see me for some reason?"

"I did. I'd like you to deliver my baby."

She had his complete attention.

"That is, if you still want to."

Ryan did. He owed it to JT. For not only his life when they had been pinned down, but because he had made a new start because of him. He had left the army, become a midwife and moved to Australia. Death was no longer a daily event.

Ryan had been afraid that if he'd continued to be a medic that he would have never seen another side of life. Would have gone deeper into depression. He'd needed a change and JT had helped him see that.

That was what it had been about when he'd first asked but now, if he was truthful with himself, he wanted to be there for Phoebe and baby. They had started to matter more than he would have ever believed. "I'd be honored."

"I can't think of anyone I'd rather have."

"Thanks. So for your first official visit with me I'm going to listen to the baby's heartbeat, check your blood pressure, measure the size of the baby and check the position by feeling your belly."

"I understand." She said this more to the floor than him.

"Hey, Phoebe." She met his gaze. "Are you sure you're good with me taking over?"

"I do want you to do the delivery, it's just that this exam stuff the first time is a little…awkward."

"For both of us. So what do you say that we get it over with and go have some dinner? Why don't you lie down on the table and tell me what else you have planned for the baby's room?"

Ryan enjoyed her nervous chatter. He didn't blame her. More than once he reminded his hands not to tremble as he placed his hand on her skin and felt for the baby's position. "Well, you and the baby are doing great. You get dressed and we'll get that dinner."

"Do you invite all your patients out to eat?" she asked in a saucy tone.

"No, I do not. I save that for very special ones."

Less than half an hour later they were ordering their dinner at a café a few blocks from the hospital.

"I would have been glad to cook."

"You've done enough of that for me."

"As compared to all you have done for me?" Phoebe glared at him.

"Okay, let's not fight over who has done more." Ryan grinned back at her. "So how have you been?"

"I'm feeling fine. Just ready for this baby to get here and tired of people treating me like I can't do anything for myself. I was moving a box across the floor in my classroom the other day. It wasn't heavy but the janitor rushed to help me. On the tram on the way in a woman offered to hold my schoolbag. She said, 'Honey, isn't that too heavy for you?' I know she was just being nice but I'd like to go somewhere and enjoy being me instead of a pregnant woman."

"People are just naturally helpful when someone is carrying a baby."

The waiter brought their dinner.

"I know. But besides the baby, there's also Phoebe Taylor in here." She pointed to her chest.

He knew that too well. The sweet taste of her kiss still lingered in his memory like the fragrance of fresh-cut wood. Still, he shouldn't have stepped over that line. He owed her an apology but he couldn't bring himself to utter the words. Nothing in him regretted kissing her, not even for a second. Maybe he could show her he'd honor her decision in another way. He would show her he could be a gentleman. That she had nothing to fear on that level from him.

"Sophia really wants me at her wedding Friday evening. Would you like to go with me? We could dance the night away. I'll promise not to treat you like a pregnant woman." That was a promise he already knew he would break. He was far too attracted to her. The pregnancy hadn't even entered his mind when he'd kissed her. Still he would work not to go beyond that barrier Phoebe had erected.

At her skeptical look, he said, "No touching outside of dancing. Just friends."

"I don't know."

"Come on, Phoebe, you know you want to. Dinner and dancing. You don't want me to show up dateless, now, do you?"

She smiled at that. "I don't think you would have any trouble getting a date if you wanted one."

"It seems I'm having to work pretty hard right now to get one."

Phoebe smirked. "Okay, but only because you sound so pitiful. My dancing may be more like swaying."

"I don't mind. We'll just go and enjoy ourselves."

"All right. It may be a long time before I get to do something like that again."

"Well, every man wants to hear that kind of enthusiasm when he asks someone out."

"I didn't mean for it to sound like that. Thanks for inviting me."

The waiter stopped by the table and refilled their glasses.

"That was much better. Why don't I bring the chest of drawers and the rocker out when I come to pick you up? That's if you don't mind me dressing at your place."

"That sounds fine. I can hardly wait to see what they look like in the baby's room."

The wedding suddenly didn't seem like the drudgery that Ryan had thought it would be.

They finishing their meal talking about movies they'd enjoyed and places they would one day like to visit.

On Friday, Phoebe wasn't sure which she was looking forward to more, seeing the furniture installed in the baby's room or the evening of dancing with Ryan. Thankfully it was a school holiday so she didn't have to lose any of her leave time by being off that day.

Ryan had said she was special. She liked being special to someone and especially to him. But it wasn't something she was going to let go any further.

Ryan had taken over her care. As odd as it was, it seemed right to let him be there when the baby was born. In the last couple of weeks he had more than proved himself the compassionate and understanding person Joshua had promised he would be. She couldn't have asked for better help. And it had been cheerfully given. She liked Ryan too much. Appreciated his support. She could use all those attributes when she delivered.

He was as good as his word. Which she had learned Ryan always was. He pulled up in front of her house at three o'clock.

She stepped out onto the veranda when she saw a sports car followed by a red truck she recognized pull to the curb. Ryan stepped out of the car and waved. She strolled down the path toward him. A man almost as tall as Ryan climbed out of the truck.

"Phoebe, this is Mike. He came along to help me move the chest in."

"Hi, Mike, thanks for going out of your way to do this."

"Nice to meet you. No worries. Ryan has given me a hand a few times."

She looked at Ryan but he gave no explanation. Knowing him, he'd gone out of his way more than once to help people, yet he had no one special in his life. It was as if he was all about deeds but not about becoming emotionally involved. Did he feel the same way about her?

"Let's get these in. Phoebe and I have a wedding to attend," he said to Mike.

The two men undid the straps securing the chest and rocker in the truck bed. They carried the chest into the house.

"Show us where you want it," Ryan said to her. She followed them down the hall and into the baby's room.

She had them place it against the wall opposite the bed. "Perfect."

Ryan grinned. "I'll get the rocker."

"Thank you for your help," Phoebe told Ryan's friend as he followed Ryan out the door.

He waved an arm. "No problem, mate."

She waited there for Ryan to return.

Doing a back-and-forth maneuver, he brought the rocker through the doorway. "Where do you want it?"

"Next to the bed, I think."

He placed it where she'd suggested.

She gave the top of the chair a nudge and watched it rock.

"Aren't you going to try it?"

"Yes, I am." She promptly took a seat, placing her hands on the ends of the arms. Moving back and forth a couple of times, she looked up at him and said in a reverent tone, "It's wonderful. Just wonderful."

"I'm glad you like it."

"I do." She continued to rock and rub the arms with her hands.

"I hate to mention this but we need to get a move on or we'll be late to Sophia's wedding."

"I know. All I need to do is slip on my dress. It shouldn't take long." She pushed out of the chair with obvious reluctance.

"My suit is in the car. Mind if I change in the other bedroom?"

"Make yourself at home," Phoebe said, as she walked out of the room. She stopped and faced him. "Ryan, it's really nice to have you around. You have been a good friend the last few weeks. I really needed one."

A lump came to Ryan's throat he couldn't clear. His heart thumped in his chest. All he could do was look at her. Before he could speak she was gone. With those few words from her he received the same high he did when he delivered a baby. That the world could be a good and kind place. Her happiness was starting to matter too much.

What had he gotten himself into? As hard as he'd worked to keep their relationship centered on helping her get ready for the baby, he'd still grown to care for the fascinating and fabulous woman that was the mother. If he wasn't careful he could become far too involved with Phoebe. Start to care too much. Did he have that in him?

He'd dressed and was waiting in the living room for Phoebe when she entered, carrying her shoes. She wore a modest sleeveless pale blue dress that had pleats in front. Her hair was down but she had pulled one side of it away from her face. It was held in place with a sparkling clasp. She was beautiful in her simplicity.

"I hate to ask this but could you help me buckle

my shoes? I've been working for five minutes to figure out how to do it around this baby and it's just not working."

Ryan smiled. "Have a seat and I'll give it a try."

She sat on the sofa and Ryan went down on one knee.

"You look like Prince Charming, dressed in your suit."

"More like a shoe salesman."

They both laughed.

She handed him a shoe and he lifted her foot and put it on.

Working with the small buckle, he said, "No wonder you were having such a hard time. This would be difficult for an aerospace engineer."

"Yes, but they look good."

Ryan rolled his eyes.

"Let's get the other one on. Man went to the moon with less effort than I'm putting into this."

She gave his shoulder a playful slap. "Remind me not to ask you for help again."

He gave her a pointed look. "And your plan for getting these off is?"

She smiled. "You are now acting like a shoe salesman and not Prince Charming."

He finished the task and stood. "Just so you'll

recognize it, this is the part where I am Prince Charming." He reached out both hands.

Phoebe put hers in his and he pulled her up until she stood. Ryan continued to hold her hands as he stepped back and studied her. "You look beautiful."

She blinked and a dreamy smile spread across her face. "Thank you. That was very Prince Charming-ish. You look very dashing yourself."

He chuckled. A ripple of pride went through him at her praise. "I do try."

She removed her hands from his and went across the room to where a shawl and purse lay in the chair nearest the front door. "We should go."

"Yes, we should. It's an hour's drive and I've not been there before."

"I know how to get there. I've been by Overnewton Castle many times. I've always wanted to go there for afternoon tea but never have been in."

"Well, princess, this is your chance." Ryan opened the door.

As she went out onto the veranda she said, "Yeah, like I look like a princess. More like a duck."

Not to me.

CHAPTER SEVEN

PHOEBE HAD HEARD that Overnewton Castle was gorgeous but she'd never imagined it was anything like this magnificent. As Ryan drove up the tree-lined drive, the Victorian Tudor-style house came into view. It resembled a castle with its textured masonry, steep roofs and turrets. The multiple stories of corners and angles covered in ivy made it look even more impressive. The expanse of rolling hills and river below created a view that was breathtaking. It was a fairy-tale spot to hold a wedding or a princess for the evening.

"Wow, what a place," Ryan said, as he pulled into the car park that was secluded by trees. "After getting engaged in a hot-air balloon, I shouldn't be surprised that Sophia and Aiden would pick a place like this to marry."

"You don't like it?"

"Sure. It's just a little over the top for me."

"I love it." She did rather feel like a princess,

being out with Ryan with the beautiful house as a backdrop.

He came around and helped her out. "I'm more like a beside-the-creek kind of guy but I have to admit this is a nice place."

"Getting married beside a creek, with the water washing over the rock, does sound nice." She pulled the shawl closer around her. When she had trouble adjusting it Ryan removed it, untwisted it and placed it across her shoulders once more. His hands lingered warm and heavy on her shoulders for a second. She missed his touch the instant it was gone.

"I think it's more about making a commitment and less about having a wedding."

Worry entered her voice. "You don't think Sophia and Aiden will last?"

"I'm not saying that. I think they'll do fine. It's just that I was in the service with too many guys whose wives had to have these big weddings and the marriages didn't last two years." He took her arm and placed it through his, putting his other hand over hers. She felt protected. Something that had been missing in her life for too long. They walked in the direction of the house.

"I had no idea you were such a cynic."

Ryan shrugged. "Maybe I am, but I just know what I've seen."

Her foot faltered on the stone path and he steadied her by pulling her against him. They continued down the path until it opened into a grassy area where white chairs had been arranged for the ceremony. Surrounding the area were trees, green foliage and brightly blooming flowers. It was a cozy place for a garden wedding.

"This must be the place." Ryan led her through the hedge opening.

Men and women stood in small groups between the house and the ceremony area. Phoebe recognized a few staff members from the hospital. An unsure feeling washed over her. Should she be here?

"Something wrong?" Ryan asked, as they made their way across the garden.

He always seemed to know when she was disturbed. She pulled away from him. "Are you sure you should have brought me? These are the people you work with and I'm not one of them."

"Look at me, Phoebe." She did. His gaze was intense. "I wanted you here with me." He took her hand. "I want to introduce you to some people I work with."

With Ryan beside her she was capable of facing anything. Phoebe had no doubt that he would remain beside her. She could rely on him. What it all came back to was that she could trust him. He would be there for her. This was the kind of relationship she'd been looking for, dreamed of. A man who would stand beside her. She glanced at his profile, and smiled.

Phoebe recognized a number of the guests from their pictures on the wall of the clinic but there was no reason that they would know her. She had only been a patient of Sophia, and now Ryan. Still, were they surprised to see him show up with a pregnant date?

She pulled on Ryan's hand, bringing him to a stop. "In that case, we both need to look our best. Let me straighten your tie."

"What's wrong with my tie?"

"It just needs an adjustment." Phoebe stepped so close that the baby brushed against him as she reached up to move his tie a centimeter to the left. "Now it's perfect."

Their gazes met.

"No, *you're* perfect." She blinked. His low raspy voice sent a ripple of awareness through her.

"Thank you," she said softly, "and thanks for this evening. It's already been wonderful." She meant that with all her heart.

His brow arched. "We haven't done anything yet."

"I know, but it was nice just to be invited out." *And to be treated as someone special.*

The group opened up as they approached to include them. Ryan went around the circle, introducing everyone. His hand came to rest on the curve of her back. "And this is my friend, Phoebe Taylor."

She noticed that Ryan had presented her as a friend when he'd only introduced the people he worked with as his colleagues. It seemed as if he didn't have many people he considered friends. Yet he and she had formed what she would call a friendship. Why didn't he have more of them?

Ryan was acting nothing like he had the day she had met him. Was he hiding from the world for some reason? What had happened?

She smiled and listened to the conversation and

banter between the members of the group. Ryan wasn't left out. He was obviously liked so why didn't he consider any of them his friends?

A few minutes later the notes from a harp sounded to announce it was time for the ceremony to begin. People started taking their seats.

"Sophia has pulled out all the stops for this wedding. I don't believe I've ever been to one with someone playing the harp," Ryan whispered. His breath brushed her neck as they stood in line, waiting for the usher to seat them.

Shivers ran down her spine. Thankfully her reaction went unnoticed because a tuxedo-wearing groomsman approached. He offered his arm and escorted her down the aisle, with Ryan following.

As they took their seats Ryan spoke to a couple of women sitting behind them. One he introduced as Isla, the head midwife in the maternity unit, and her husband, Dr. Alessandro Manos, who was one of the doctors there. Phoebe recognized Isla from visits to the clinic. A number of times Phoebe had seen her in the hallway. She was also very familiar with the prominent Delamere name. It appeared often in the society pages. She and Isla had something in common. Isla was pregnant as well but not as far along as she was. The other woman was Dr. Darcie Green. Phoebe was told she was a visiting obstetrician from London but she didn't catch her date's name.

After they were settled in their chairs she glanced at Ryan. He wore a stoic look. She leaned toward him. "This really isn't your favorite thing to do, is it?"

His shoulder touched hers. They must have looked like two lovers whispering. What would it be like to be loved by Ryan? Amazing would be her guess. She'd sworn to herself she wouldn't cross the line, had made Ryan pledge the same, but she wasn't sure she wanted it that way any longer.

"Do you know a man that enjoys this?"

She paused. "No, I guess not. We don't have to stay."

"I promised dinner and dancing and I don't plan to disappoint you." Ryan moved closer, putting his mouth to her ear. The intimacy made her grow warm. "*Men* do like food and holding women."

Was he looking forward to dancing with her as much as she was look forward to spending time in his arms? Thankfully, a woman stood in front and began to sing a hymn, leaving Phoebe no more time to contemplate the anticipation of having Ryan hold her. She wasn't sure she could have commented if she'd had a chance. Minutes later the parents of the bride and groom were seated. The harpist played again. The groom and groomsmen stepped to the altar, which was defined by a white metal arch.

Phoebe straightened her back as far as she could to see over the heads of those sitting in front of them. The men wore black tuxedos, making them look not only dashing but sophisticated. She glanced at Ryan and imagined what he would look like in a tux. Very handsome, no doubt. She could only see the top of the best man's head. He was in a wheelchair.

Ryan put his arm across the back of her chair and whispered, "That's Aiden's brother, Nathan, in the chair."

Phoebe nodded.

The harpist continued to play as the bridesmaids came down the aisle. They were dressed in bright yellow knee-length dresses of various styles. Each carried a bouquet of white daisies.

As they joined the men, they made a striking combination against the backdrop of trees and plants.

A breeze picked up and Phoebe pulled her wrap closer. She felt Ryan adjusting the wrap to cover her right arm completely. His hand rested on her shoulder. There was something reassuring about the possessive way he touched her.

She looked at him and smiled.

It was time for Sophia to come down the aisle. At the first note of the traditional wedding march everyone stood. Phoebe went up on her toes to catch a glimpse of the bride going by.

"Move so I can see." She nudged Ryan back a step so she could peer around him.

He gave her an indulgent smile and complied.

What little she could observe of Sophia looked beautiful. When she reached Aiden all the guests sat.

Ryan's hand came to rest on her shoulder again. He nudged her close. "You really do like this stuff."

"Shush," Phoebe hissed.

He chuckled softly.

It wasn't long until Sophia and Aiden were coming back down the aisle as man and wife.

Ryan took Phoebe's hand as they filed out of their row. He continued to hold it while they walked across the garden toward the house where the reception would be held. They entered the main hall through glass doors. Cocktails and hors d'oeuvres were being served there. Phoebe gasped at the beauty of the majestic circular staircase before them. It and the dark wood paneling were all the decoration required.

"Come over here," Ryan said, placing his hand on her waist. "If you plan to dance the night away, I think you need to get off your feet and rest while you can."

For once she accepted his concern and consideration. She'd gone so many years doing everything for herself that having someone think of her was fabulous. This evening she was going to enjoy being pampered. Having it done by Ryan would be even nicer.

There were high-backed chairs sitting along the wall and she took one of them. Ryan stood beside her. When the waiter carrying drinks came by they both requested something nonalcoholic, she because she was pregnant and he because he said he would be driving. She liked it that he was acting responsibly. Now that she was having a baby it seemed she thought about that more.

A number of people stopped and spoke to Ryan. While he talked to them, his fingers lightly rested against the top of her shoulder. It would be clear to everyone that she was with him. He never failed to introduce her. A few people gave her belly a searching look and then grinned at them. They must have thought they were a couple.

"Why, hello, Ryan. I never took you for a wedding kind of guy. I've never even seen you at a Christmas party." The words were delivered in a teasing tone by a woman who joined them.

Phoebe looked up at Ryan and he seemed to take the comment in stride.

"Hello, Vera. It's nice to see you, too. Sophia twisted my arm on this one. Couldn't get out of it. I'd like you to meet Phoebe Taylor." He directed the next statement to Phoebe. "Vera is the hospital's chief anesthetist."

"Hi." Phoebe smiled at Vera.

"Nice to meet you." Vera's attention went back

to Ryan. "I had no idea you were expecting a baby."

"It's not mine."

"Oh." She made the word carry a mountain of suggestions and questions.

"Phoebe was a wife of a friend of mine in the service. He was killed eight months ago."

Vera looked down at Phoebe. "I'm sorry."

"Thank you." Somehow the pain of Joshua not being there had eased over the last few weeks.

"So when's the baby due?"

"In just a few weeks," Phoebe said.

"You're being followed at Victoria antenatal?" Vera showed true interest.

"You mean prenatal," Ryan quipped.

She glared at him. "I wished you'd get away from calling it that. I have to think twice when you do."

"And I have to think when you called it antenatal. Old habits die hard."

"I guess they do. Well, I'd better mingle. Nice to meet you, Phoebe."

"Bye." Once again Ryan had proved that he was well liked and respected. So why didn't he socialize with his colleagues?

A few minutes later the guests were called to dinner. On a table outside the room was a place card with Ryan's name on it and a table number. He picked it up and led the way.

The room was stunning. Round tables with white tablecloths covering them to the floor filled it. Chairs were also covered in white with matching bows on the back. At the front of the room, facing the guests, was one long table for the bridal party.

By the time they arrived at their table, Isla and Darcie, the two women who had sat behind them during the ceremony, were already there. Ryan took the chair next to Darcie, and Phoebe sat on his other side. Another couple who knew Isla joined them and took the last seats. Everyone introduced themselves. Most of Phoebe's time was spent talking to the woman beside her. Occasionally, someone across the table would ask a question but hearing was difficult with the amount of chatter in the room.

The bridal party was introduced and Sophia and Aiden took their places before the meal was served. The noise dropped as people ate.

"So, Phoebe," Isla asked from directly across the table, "when's your baby due?"

That was the most popular question of the evening. "In a couple of weeks."

"Are you being seen in the MMU?"

"I am. Sophia was my midwife but she thought falling in love was more important." Phoebe smiled.

"That does happen. Who's following you now?"

"That would be me," Ryan announced. There was a note of pride in his voice.

A hush came over the table. Phoebe didn't miss the looks of shock on the two women's faces. Was something wrong? She glanced at Ryan. It wasn't a secret. Why should it be?

"Phoebe needed someone and I volunteered," Ryan offered, as he picked up his water glass and took a sip.

Both women looked from him, then back to her and back again. Ryan didn't seem fazed by their reaction.

Finally Isla said, "Ryan's one of the best. You'll be happy with his care."

After they had eaten their meal, Ryan watched Phoebe make her way to the restroom. His attention was drawn away from her when Isla sat down in Phoebe's place.

Isla leaned close and hissed, "Just what do you think you're doing?"

He sat back, surprised by her aggression. "Doing?"

Darcie moved in from the other side, sandwiching him in. "You're dating a patient!"

"I am not."

"What do you call it when you bring the woman you're going to deliver for to a wedding as your date?" Isla asked.

"I call it dating," Darcie quipped.

"Look, Phoebe is the widow of a service buddy of mine. All I'm trying to do is be her friend. She doesn't have anyone else."

"That wasn't a friendly arm around her at the ceremony. Or a friendly look just a second ago when she walked away," Isla stated, as if she were giving a lecture to a first-year student.

"Or when you were looking at her as she fixed your tie," Darcie added.

"You saw that?" Ryan was amazed. They had seen what he'd believed he'd been covering well—his attraction to Phoebe.

"Yes, we…" Darcie indicated her date "…went past you and you didn't even see us, you were so engrossed."

"I was not."

"You can deny it all you want but I'm telling you what I saw. The point here is that you shouldn't be dating a patient. It's bad form and if someone wanted to make a big deal of it you might lose your job." Isla looked around as if she was checking to see if anyone was listening.

Ryan chuckled. "You're overreacting to two friends spending an evening together."

"I still say you better be careful. You're stepping over the line with this one," Isla said.

Darcie nodded her agreement.

He leaned back and looked at one then the other. "Well, are either one of you going to report me?"

The two women looked at each other. Both shook their heads.

"Thank you. I asked Phoebe to come with me because she's had a rough year, finding out her husband was killed and then that she was pregnant. This was her big night out before the baby comes. In any case, all of that about me delivering the baby will be a moot point in a few weeks. So, ladies, I appreciate your concern but I'm going to show Phoebe a pleasant evening and if that looks bad to you I'm sorry."

They grinned at each other.

"You were right, Isla. He does care about her." Darcie smirked.

Isla patted him on the shoulder. "Good luck."

Ryan wasn't sure what that meant but it was better than being reprimanded for something he didn't believe was a problem.

Phoebe returned, and Isla moved back to her chair and kissed her husband on the cheek as she sat down. She smiled at Phoebe.

After Phoebe sat she leaned over and whispered, "Is everything all right?"

He took her hand beneath the table, gave it a squeeze and held it. "Everything is great."

Dessert had been served by the time the bride and groom started around the room, greeting their guests. When they reached Phoebe and Ryan's table Sophia hugged each person in turn until she worked her way to Ryan.

"Well, I'm glad to see you. I wasn't sure you'd be here."

Ryan hugged Sophia in return. "O ye of little faith."

She laughed and turned to Phoebe. For a second there was a look of astonishment on Sophia's face when she saw her but it soon disappeared. "Phoebe, I'm so glad to see you. I'd like you to meet my husband, Aiden."

While Phoebe spoke to Aiden, Ryan didn't miss the look that passed between Sophia, Isla and Darcie.

Did his feelings for Phoebe really show that much? They must if they were that obvious to the three women. How had he let it happen? He glanced at Phoebe. The devil of it was, he hadn't. All it took was just being around Phoebe to make him care. And that he did far too much.

She giggled at something Sophia said. He wanted her too much. There was little that was professional about his feelings. How would she take it when he told her that he could no longer be her midwife?

The strains of an orchestra tuning up came from somewhere in the house.

Sophia's father asked everyone to join them for

dancing and a toast to the bride and groom in the solarium. Ryan took her hand as they made their way there. It was as if he didn't want to break the contact with her. She didn't want to, either.

Phoebe had been sure that what she'd already seen of the castle couldn't be surpassed, but she'd been wrong. Two-thirds of the solarium consisted of glass walls and glass ceiling. It had turned dark and small lights above created a magical place.

Ryan directed her to one of the café-size tables stationed around the room. They sat and watched the bride and groom dance their first dance. The staff saw to it that everyone had a glass of champagne to toast the couple. Ryan smiled as he tapped her glass. Phoebe took the smallest sip and set the glass down. His joined hers on the table. The orchestra began to play again.

Ryan stood and offered his hand. "It's time I made good on my promise. Would you care to dance?"

"Why, sir, I think I would." Phoebe smiled at him and placed her hand in his.

"I'll have to tell you that I'm not a very good

dancer," Ryan said, as he led her out on to the floor.

She laughed. "Have you looked at me lately? I'm not very graceful so I don't think it'll matter if you're a good dancer or not."

"Then I guess we're the perfect match."

Were they really?

Ryan took her into his arms, holding her close as they moved around the floor. He'd touched her before but had never put his arms completely around her. It was lovely to have him so close. He smelled like a warm forest after a spring rain. She leaned in and inhaled. Wonderful.

The overhead lights were turned low and the tiny ones became more brilliant. They slowly swayed to the music. Did fairy tales really come true? Phoebe had no idea if they were with the beat or not. It didn't matter. The next song was a faster one and they separated. She felt the loss of Ryan's warmth immediately and her body waited impatiently to have it returned. Not allowing her to completely lose contact, he continued to hold one of her hands. As soon as the faster dance was over, he brought her back into his embrace. Her fingers rested on his shoulders and his found her waist. As they moved slowly, they looked into each other's eyes. Something was occurring here that she'd never planned, never thought would happen. She was falling in love.

"Does dancing with me make you think of that game you might have played in gym class where you had to keep a ball between you and your partner without using your hands?"

He stopped moving. "How's that?"

"Dancing with the baby between us."

Ryan laughed. "I had skill at that game. Always won." He pulled her closer. "You're the best partner I've ever had."

Her hand cupped his face. "You're a nice guy."

Ryan's eyes grew intense and he cleared his throat. "It's warm in here. Why don't we go outside for a few minutes?"

She nodded. He led her through a half-hidden glass door that looked like part of the wall, onto a brick patio.

"It feels good out here." Phoebe breathed in the cold evening air. The music from inside drifted around them. It was painfully romantic. Was Ryan feeling the same need?

"It does." Ryan stood a couple of steps away, just out of touching distance.

She wanted his touch. Wanted to feel desired. It had been too long. Even with Joshua the last time she hadn't felt desire. Sex had become more of an obligation, expectation than anything else. There should be more than that in a relationship. There was with Ryan. Would he think she was too forward if she reached for him?

A wide set of steps led to a pond below. Surrounding it was an extensive grassy area. The lights of the solarium reflected off the water, making the view even more dreamlike. Phoebe started down the steps.

"Where're you going?" Ryan asked.

"I thought I'd stand in the garden and admire the solarium." She was already watching the others dance when Ryan joined her.

"It reminds me of a carousel music box I once had as a child. As it played, horses with people riding them went by in shadow. It was like watching something magical. I could look at it for hours. I loved it," she whispered, as much to herself as to him.

"You are a romantic." He now stood close

enough that his arm brushed hers as their fingers intertwined.

"Because I think there can be fairy tales?"

He didn't say anything for a while. "I haven't believed in fairy tales for a long time, but somehow when I'm around you they do seem possible."

"I know you've lived through some horrible things you can't seem to leave behind, but you need to know there's good in life, too. Happy times that can replace the bad. Like this baby. Joshua is gone, yet in a way he's bringing new life into the world. Something good for me."

"Good can be hard to find."

His fingers tightened. Phoebe glanced at him. He stood rigid, as if the discussion was painful for him. His gaze met hers and she said, "It can be. And it can come from unexpected places, too."

"Like you?"

"I like to think so but I wasn't talking about me so much as from friends and family. Finding people that matter to you. Letting them know they are important to you."

"I can't do that."

She stepped closer, her body touching his. "I think you can. In fact, I know you can. You've been a friend to me these last few weeks."

They continued to stand there, not saying a word. It wasn't until the doors were opened wide by the Overnewton staff members that the spell was broken and they broke apart. The crowd poured out of the solarium and began lining up along the steps.

"I guess it's time for Sophia and Aiden to leave," Phoebe murmured.

"We should join everyone." Ryan didn't sound like he really wanted to. Had their conversation put a dampener on the evening? She would hate that to happen. Had she ever enjoyed a wedding more?

As they stood at the bottom of the steps, a gust of wind caught her shawl. She shivered and pulled it closer.

"You're cold." Ryan removed his jacket and placed it over her shoulders. It still held his body heat. His scent. She pulled it tighter around her.

Someone near passed them each a small container of bird seed. As Sophia and Aiden descended the steps they were showered with the seed for good luck. When they reached Phoebe and Ryan, Aiden whisked Sophia into his arms and carried her to a waiting car.

Phoebe looked down at her expanded middle. "I'd like to see someone whisk me up like that."

Suddenly her feet were in the air and she was being held against a hard chest. "Oh."

Her arms went around Ryan's neck. He swung her around a few times. She giggled.

Ryan put her on her feet again. "I didn't see it as a problem."

As he smiled down at her, a tingle grew low within her from the warmth she saw in his eyes. She glanced around. Some of the crowd was watching them. She didn't care. What she wanted was to help make Ryan see that fairy tales could come true. He had the biggest heart of anyone she knew, loyal, caring and generous. With a wicked sense of humor that only made her love him more. That's what she felt. Love for him. She'd fallen under his spell. He wasn't going to leave her. More than once he'd proved he'd be there when she needed him. She could depend on him.

Phoebe's hands remained about his neck. She looked up into his eyes and smiled. "That was fun."

"I think it's time for us to go." He looked down at her, his voice coming out soft and raspy.

Ryan walked Phoebe to her door. She'd been quiet on their drive home. Had she been thinking about those moments when they had looked into each other's eyes? He'd known then there was no going back. He wanted her and she wanted him. It had been there in her crystal clear look of assurance.

As he'd pulled out onto the main road, he'd taken her hand and rested it on his thigh. She hadn't resisted. For once she hadn't fallen asleep during the drive. Had she been as keyed up as he'd been? He wanted her but he couldn't lead her on. Have her believe there was more than just a physical attraction between them.

Her hand had remained in his the entire way back to Box Hill. She had asked for his help with her shoes when they'd arrived at his car. He had obliged. When they'd arrived at her house she'd stepped out of the car carrying them by two fingers.

They walked to her front porch. "It was a perfect evening, Ryan. Thank you so much for inviting me."

"I'm glad you had a good time. Mine wouldn't have been near as nice if you'd not gone with me."

She fumbled with her purse.

"Hand those to me." Ryan indicated the shoes. She found her keys and unlocked the door, pushing it open. Ryan followed her in.

"Would you like some coffee?" Phoebe dropped her shoes beside the door.

"I thought you didn't drink coffee."

She turned to look at him. "I don't. I bought it for you."

"Then, yes, I would." It had been a long time since someone had bought anything especially for him. It meant she thought about him even when he wasn't around. That idea he liked far too much.

He followed her to the kitchen. He leaned against the door frame and watched as Phoebe put a kettle of water on a burner. He was fascinated by the combination of her in a beautiful dress with bare feet, preparing coffee. There was something so domestic about the picture that it made him want to run as far away from there as he could get while at the same time it pulled him in, making him wish for more, had him longing for someone special in his life.

Phoebe stood on her toes to reach the bag of coffee. Her dress rose enough that he had a view of the backs of her knees and thighs. An impulse to run a hand along all that skin and under her dress made his pants tighten. Heaven help him, he wanted her so badly. Right here, right now. The entire evening had been leading up to this moment. From the time he'd was on his knee, helping her put her shoes on, until now he'd known he had to have her.

He should walk away. Go out the door without a word said. The gentleman in him, the professional, screamed for him to leave. But he wouldn't. The temptation to kiss her was too great. Unable to resist, he closed the small distance between them. Pushing her hair away, he kissed her neck. He pressed his front to her back, letting his desire be known. "I know what I agreed to, but I can't stop myself. I want you."

Before he could say more, she pushed back against him, gaining enough room to face him. She wrapped her hands around his waist and lifted her face. Her eyes were clear and confident. The quiver of her lips gave him a hint of what this boldness was costing her. Still, she was offering.

Slowly his mouth met hers.

A flood of disappointment went through him when she pulled away seconds later but quickly turned into a storm of longing as Phoebe's lips met his again. They were soft and mobile. Small cushions of bliss. This was better than he remembered. He wanted more.

Ryan reached around her and turned off the burner, then pulled her closer. He brought his lips more fully against hers.

Phoebe's hands moved to grip his biceps. She shifted, pressing her breasts to his chest.

The arousal he felt at the first touch of her lips grew, lengthened. Hardened. His mouth released hers and moved across her cheek. He left a trail of butterfly kisses on his way to the sweet spot behind her ear. Phoebe moaned, then tilted her head so that he could better reach her neck. She snuggled against him.

The desire to have her made his muscles draw tight. He wanted her here. Now. His hands caressed her back and settled low on her hips. He gathered her dress in his hands and pulled her against his throbbing need.

"Phoebe, you'll have to stop us because I can't," he murmured as his mouth pressed down on hers, begging her for entrance.

Her hands went to the nape of his neck in an eager movement, pulling his lips more firmly to hers. She opened her mouth, and his tongue didn't hesitate to gain entrance. Hers met his to tease and tantalize. It was a duel of pleasure that he didn't want to win.

His body hummed with a need that only Phoebe could ease.

She pulled her mouth away.

"Aw. What's wrong?"

"The baby kicked."

Damn. He'd forgotten all about the baby. How could he? Because he was so focused on his hunger for Phoebe. He stepped back far enough that he was no longer touching her.

"I'm sorry. I didn't mean to hurt you."

"Silly, you weren't hurting me." She took a predatory step toward him. "Babies kick."

"I shouldn't, we shouldn't…"

"Come on, Ryan. We're adults. I'm certainly aware of the facts of life, and I'm sure you are, too. So we both know that what we were doing wouldn't hurt the baby. I want this. I want you. From what I could tell, you wanted me."

That would be an understatement.

"I'm going to my bedroom. I hope you join me. If not, please lock up on your way out."

She went up on the tips of her toes, kissed him and left the kitchen. Ryan stood there with his manhood aching and the choice of a lifetime to make.

How like Phoebe to be so direct. If he joined her, could he remain emotionally detached? He already cared more than he should and certainly more than he was comfortable with. But if he didn't, he would never know the heaven of being with Phoebe. There was no decision. A beautiful, desirable woman that he wanted was offering him the world. There was no question of whether or not to accept.

CHAPTER EIGHT

PHOEBE SAT ON the edge of the bed in her room. A lone lamp burned on her bedside table. She'd never been so brazen in her life. But how else was she going to get through to Ryan? She wanted him desperately. Needed his calm caring, his reliability and assurance in her life. It was so quiet in the house that she feared he'd slipped out and gone home. Seconds later her heart thumped against her ribs at the sound of footfalls in the hallway.

He'd stayed.

Ryan hesitated at the door. Their gazes met, held. He removed his tie and jacket and dropped them over the chair, then he stalked across the floor and pulled her to her feet and into his arms.

This was where she belonged.

His mouth met hers. She opened for him. Their tongues mated in a frenzied battle of touch and retreat. Heat flowed through her, strong and sure, pooling low in her. Ryan's lips left hers and he buried his face in her neck. He nipped at her skin. The desire that flickered in her blazed.

He gathered her dress along one leg, sliding a hand under the fabric. She hissed as his fingers touched her skin. His hand glided around her leg until it found the inside of her thigh and squeezed lightly. She shivered.

Ryan removed his hand. He met her gaze. Placing his hands on her shoulders, he turned her around.

"What…?"

"Shush," he all but growled. He gathered her hair, running his fingers through it. "Beautiful," he murmured, before placing it over a shoulder.

There was a tug at the top of her dress. He opened the zipper. The tug ended and his lips found the skin between her shoulder blades. A shudder traveled down her spine. His mouth skimmed over each vertebra to her waist. There he spent some time kissing and touching with the tip of his tongue the curve of her back.

She began to move but he said, "Not yet."

Ryan's fingertip followed the same path upward, then his palms until he brushed her dress off her shoulders. She crossed her arms, preventing the dress from falling away from her breasts.

He kissed the length of the ridge between her neck and arm. "So silky."

Phoebe sighed. This was too wonderful. "Let me turn off the lamp."

He guided her to face him. "Phoebe, look at me."

Her eyes rose to meet his gaze.

"You're beautiful." He placed his hands on either side of the baby. "That's a new life you're carrying. There's nothing more amazing or natural than that. Please don't hide it from me."

If she could have melted she would have. "You're sure?"

"Honey, I'm more than sure." Ryan moved closer to bring his taught length against her belly, leaving her in no doubt of his desire.

It was an empowering thought to know that was all for her.

Stepping back, he took both her hands and opened her arms. The dress fell away, leaving her breasts visible, cupped in a lacy pink bra. Her dress gathered on her belly. Ryan gave it a gentle tug at the seams and the dress pooled around her feet on the floor.

His gaze fixed on her breasts. He sucked in a breath and she crossed her arms again.

"Please, don't. You're amazing. I want to admire you."

"They're so large." She couldn't look at him.

Ryan lifted her chin with a finger until her gaze met his. "I don't know a man in the world who doesn't love large breasts. Especially if they are his to admire."

The heat building in her grew. Ryan knew how to make her feel beautiful.

He removed her arms. Using a finger, he followed the cleft of her cleavage. Her nipples pushed against her bra as they swelled. A tingle zipped through her breasts. His finger traced the line of her bra first over one mound and then the other. She swayed and Ryan slipped an arm around her.

With a deft movement of his fingers he unclipped her bra. He slipped it off one arm. His tongue followed the same path as his finger. On the return trip, he veered off. At the same time his free hand lifted her right breast, his mouth captured her nipple.

Her womb contracted. "Ryan…" she muttered. She wasn't sure if she was begging for him to stop or to continue.

Ryan supported her as she leaned back, offering herself completely to him. Her hands went to his shoulders in the hope she could steady her body and her emotions. His mouth slid to the other nipple. Her fingertips bit into his shoulders.

Ryan's hand traced the line of her undies until he reached her center. It brushed her mound and retreated. Her center throbbed with the need for him to return. Using the arm around her waist, he pulled her toward him until she was no longer leaning back. His hand swept the other strap of her bra off and down her arm, letting the undergarment drop to the floor.

She looked at him. Ryan's gaze was fixed on her breasts. His hand reached up and stopped millimeters from her nipple. It had the slightest tremor to it. She would have missed it if she hadn't been watching. They both understood the facts of life well and still these moments of passion were overwhelming. He touched the tip of her nipple with the end of his finger.

Something similar to lightning shot through her.

"So responsive," Ryan murmured in a note of satisfaction as he ran a finger gently over her skin. It was as if a breeze had come through. He did the same to the other breast.

Phoebe quaked all over. There was something erotic about watching Ryan touch her. Her nerve endings tingled. She had to touch him. See his reaction.

He moved back and lifted both her breasts, kissing each one in turn. Taking a nipple in his mouth, he traced it with his tongue and tugged. She bucked against him.

"Clothes." The word came out as a strangled sound. "I want to see you."

A noise came low in his throat. Leaving a kiss on the curve of her breast, he stepped back. Undoing his tie, he jerked it from his collar and began unbuttoning his shirt.

While he did that she released his belt. She ran the back of her hand down the bulge of his manhood. His body's reaction to hers was stimulating. It gave her a boldness she'd never had before. She backed away until her legs found the side of the bed and she sat. Looking up at Ryan, she caught his gaze. "Come here. It's my turn."

His shirt fluttered to the floor. He stepped close enough for her to touch him. Finding his zipper, she slowly lowered it. Her hand moved to touch him but he stopped her by capturing her hand and bringing it to his lips. "Don't." The word sounded harsh with tension. "I don't think I can control myself if you do."

Phoebe pulled her hand from his. Sliding her hands between the waist of his pants and his hips, she pushed. His trousers fell to the floor. He wore red plaid boxers that didn't disguise his size. Ryan was no small man anywhere.

He kicked off his shoes, then finished removing his slacks. Leaning over, he jerked off his socks.

Phoebe reached out and ran her hand through his hair. Her fingers itched to gather the mass and pull him to her. Had she ever been this turned on? She wanted Ryan beside her, on her and in her like she'd never wanted before. Her hands slowly slipped from his hair and Ryan looked at her. He nudged her back on the bed and came down beside her.

"I want to touch you like you did me." Phoebe rolled to her side.

He faced her.

Her heart leaped at his unspoken agreement. The lovemaking between Joshua and her had always been fast and desperate, never slow and passionate, as she was experiencing now.

Ryan wasn't sure he could stand much more of Phoebe's administering. As it was, he gritted his teeth to control his need to dive into her.

Her index finger traced the line of his lips. He captured the end and drew it into his mouth and sucked. Her eyes darkened. She slowly removed her finger. His manhood flinched. Did she have any idea how erotic she was?

Phoebe's small hand ran down the side of his neck in a gentle motion. It glided over his shoulder. She placed a kiss there. Her hair hid her face as it flowed over his skin like silk. He couldn't resist touching it, watching it move through his fingers. Pushing it away from her face, he cupped her cheek and brought her lips to his. She eagerly accepted. Her hands fluttered across his chest, moving up to the nape of his neck.

When he leaned over to take the kiss deeper, Phoebe pushed against his shoulders, breaking the connection. One hand at his neck dropped lower to run across his chest. She took an infinite amount of time tracing each of his ribs. As if she was trying to commit each curve, dip and rise of him to memory. His muscles quivered from the attention.

Her hand went lower, a finger dipping into his belly button. At his sharp inhalation she giggled. He loved the sound. Her hand moved to his side and rubbed up and down it to return to his stomach. She smoothed her fingers over his hip. The tips slipped under the elastic band of his boxers and retreated just as quickly.

Phoebe rose enough to accommodate the baby and kissed the center of his chest. At the same time her fingers went deeper under his boxers than before, touching the tip of his manhood.

Only with a force of control he hadn't known he possessed did he manage not to lose it.

Pulling her back, he gathered her to him and kissed her with a depth of need he was afraid to examine. She clung to him as if she never wanted to let him go.

"Phoebe, I need you now."

"I'm here."

Ryan scooted off the bed and removed his boxers. Phoebe's intake of breath made his manhood rise. He held out his hand and she took it, standing. His hands found the waistband of her undies and slipped them down her legs. She stepped out of them. He flipped the covers back to the end of the bed. Phoebe climbed in and seconds later he had her in his arms again.

"I don't want to hurt you. Or the baby."

She met his direct look with one of her own. "You would never do that."

The confidence she had in him shook him to the core. This wouldn't just be a physical joining but an emotional one, as well. He'd never intended to care but he did.

Ryan shifted to the center of the bed, then brought her over him until she straddled his waist. On her knees above him, her beautiful full breasts hung down like juicy melons, tempting him to feast. He wasted no time in doing so. As he savored all that was offered, Phoebe shifted so that her entrance teased his length. It ached in anticipation of finding home.

Phoebe kissed him as he lifted her hips and positioned her on him. He slid into her and they became one. He held his breath. It wasn't he but she who moved first. He joined her. Using his hands, he helped control their movements. At her frustrated sound he eased his grip and she settled farther down on him.

His hands remained lightly on her as he guided her up and down again and again. She was a beauty with her golden hair hanging down, her eyes closed and her head thrown back. With a shudder and a hiss of pleasure, she looked at him and gave him a dreamy smile.

Yes, he was the king of the world.

He kissed her deeply and flexed his hips against hers. After two powerful thrusts he found his own bliss.

Phoebe rolled off Ryan. Her head came to rest on his arm, a hand on his chest, her baby between them. She wished it would always be this way. She loved Ryan. He cared for her. She had no doubt of that. His lovemaking proved it. But would he ever admit it to himself or her that he might want something lasting? It didn't matter, it wouldn't change how she felt.

She yawned. "I'm tired."

Ryan grinned. "Me, too. For a pregnant lady you sure can be rough on a man."

"So what you're saying is that you're not man enough for me."

Ryan pulled her to him for a kiss that curled her toes. His already growing manhood pushed against her leg.

"You need me to prove I'm man enough?"

"No, I think you did that just fine a few minutes ago. Right now, I need to rest. Too much dining, dancing and man." Her eyes closed to the feel of Ryan's hand rubbing her back.

Phoebe woke to the sun streaming through the bedroom window. She was alone. Panic filled her. Had Ryan left?

A clang came from the direction of the kitchen. She'd woken once during the night. Her back had been against his solid chest and his hand had cupped her right breast. It had been a perfect night. She wanted more of them.

He'd said nothing about how he felt. He had been an attentive and caring lover. She had never felt more desired. Still, she might be reading more into his actions than there was.

"Hey, I was hoping you were still asleep." Ryan walked into the room with a smile on his face and carrying a tray.

Phoebe pulled the sheet up to cover her chest. "Good morning to you, too. What do you have there?"

"It's supposed to be your breakfast in bed."

She'd never had anyone feed her in bed. Sitting up, she peered at the tray. "Really? That sounds nice."

He didn't seem to feel any morning-after awkwardness. She would be happy to follow his lead. Her biggest fear the night before had been that she would be a disappointment because of her size. The second fear had been that there would be unease between them this morning. Ryan had made it clear he wasn't turned off by her body. By his actions so far this morning, he was the same Ryan he had been last night.

He sat the tray at the end of the bed. She recognized it as one off the table in her living room.

On it was sliced apples, two bowls of cereal and two glasses of orange juice.

"Lean forward."

Phoebe did as he asked. Ryan stuffed pillows behind her and she settled back. He joined her on the bed.

"No bacon and eggs?" She added a mock pout. "Afraid you'd burn yourself?

"You're so funny. I did what I was capable of doing. We can have something more substantial later."

"This looks wonderful to me."

She kissed him on the cheek.

"That wasn't much of a thank-you kiss. I think you can do better." His lips found hers. Seconds later Phoebe wanted to forget about their breakfast and concentrate on nothing but Ryan. Her arms went around his neck and she pulled him closer.

Ryan broke the kiss. "We need to be careful or we'll have juice and cereal everywhere. As much as I'd like to go on kissing you, I know you need nutrition."

"That sounded very midwife-ish."

He lowered his chin and gave her a serious look. "Well, that's what I am."

"And you are mine."

He was hers. Ryan liked the sound of that but he could never be what she needed. He couldn't commit to being hers, like she deserved. He wasn't who she thought he was. She should have someone who could love her wholeheartedly, holding nothing back. He had to see to it that their relationship remained light and easy. But after what had happened between them last night, that might be impossible.

"As your medical professional, I say eat."

"Can I put something on first?"

"I don't mind you the way you are." He grinned.

"That's sweet of you to say but I think I'd be less self-conscious with my gown on. After all, you have your underwear on."

Ryan stood. "Okay, if it'll get you to eat something, tell me where your gowns are."

She pointed to a chest. "Second drawer."

He didn't make a habit of going through a woman's personal things and found it almost too much like they were in a lifelong relationship to do so in Phoebe's. As quickly as he could, he pulled out a light blue gown. Returning to her, he helped her slip it over her head. Sitting on the edge of the bed, he asked, "Satisfied now?"

"Yes, I'm not used to breakfast in bed and I'm sure not used to sharing it with someone when I have no clothes on."

"I like you naked."

"Even with this beach ball of a belly?" She touched her middle.

He kissed her. "Women are at their prettiest when they are expecting. You glow."

She gathered her hair and pulled it over one shoulder. Her chin went up and she batted her eyelashes. "I glow? I like that."

"Yes, you glow but you would be brighter if you'd eat something." Ryan pulled the tray closer and handed her a glass of juice.

They spent the next few minutes discussing the wedding, the weather and what other plans she had for the baby's room.

When they had finished eating Ryan stood, took the tray and was on his way out the door when Phoebe's squeak stopped him. He wheeled to look at her. Concern washed over him. Was something wrong? Should he take her to the hospital? "Are you okay?"

"Yes, just the baby making its presence known." She grinned. "I did have a little more activity last night than I normally do."

Relief flooded him. He needed to calm down, not overreact. Being a midwife, he should know better, but this was Phoebe. He cared for his patients but on no level did that came close to what he felt for Phoebe. How was he going to remain professional when he delivered the baby? Maybe it would be better if someone else did. "I'm sorry."

"I should hope not! Because I'm sure not."

"Thanks. My ego would have been damaged otherwise."

"I wouldn't want that to happen." She winced and shifted in the bed. "This baby is getting his morning exercise."

Ryan grinned. "I have an idea to help with those aches and pains. You stay there while I take this to the kitchen. I'll be right back. Don't move."

The anticipation of being in Ryan's arms again was enough to have Phoebe's blood humming.

He soon returned with the bottle of lotion in his hand he had used the other night during her foot massage.

"Oh, I'm going to get another foot massage." She couldn't keep the eagerness out of her voice and started moving toward the edge of the bed.

"No. Stay where you are. Just move forward some." He put the lotion on the bedside table.

Her brow wrinkled but she did as he asked. What did he have planned this time?

Ryan climbed in bed behind her, putting a leg on each side of her hips so that she now sat between his.

"What're you doing?"

There was all kind of movement behind her until Ryan's arms came around her and pulled her back against his chest. "I was having a hard time getting the pillows to stay in place. Pull your gown up."

"What is this? Some special pregnant woman's sex position?"

He chuckled behind her. "Is that all you think about? Sex?"

"When you're around, yes."

He kissed her neck. "Thank you for the nice

compliment but right now I have something else in mind. Now pull your gown up."

She did as he said until it was gathered under her breasts then adjusted the sheet over her thighs, giving her some modesty.

Ryan reached around her neck.

"Hey, is this a fancy way of choking me?"

"You sure are making it hard for me to be nice to you."

Cold hit her bare middle, making her jerk. "Ooh."

"That'll teach you not to have such a smart mouth," Ryan said in a teasing tone. His hands began to glide over her middle. "You're all tense. Lie back and enjoy."

She did, settling against his chest and closing her eyes. Ryan's hands made slow circles over her middle.

"This is wonderful. Did you learn to do this in the service, too?"

"No. But I did deliver my first baby there."

"Will you tell me about it?"

Ryan's body tensed behind her. He was quiet so long she wasn't sure he would say anything more.

"One weekend we were invited to a local celebration. I'm still not sure what it was for, but anyway some of the unit went along. We ate the food. Played with the kids.

"You know, kids are the same wherever you go. All they want is their parents there for them and to play and be happy. Every child deserves that." Ryan's hands drifted to the sides of her belly. His palms pressed lightly against her. "Especially this one."

Phoebe placed her hand over one of his. "He or she will have that. I promise."

It would be wonderful if Ryan would be a part of helping her make that come true. But he said nothing that indicated he wanted that kind of involvement in their lives.

"After the celebration we were going back to the base but had to stop because there was mechanical trouble with one of the trucks. There happened to be three or four huts that locals lived in nearby. There was a loud scream from that direction. A couple of the men went to investigate. It turned out that there was a woman having a baby. She was in trouble. They returned for me.

"I don't think I've even been in a house that had less. It was made of mud bricks, with a grass roof and dirt floor. Water was drawn from a barely running creek half a mile away. The kitchen consisted of a pot over a fire. In this horrible war-torn country, in this nothing shelter was a woman trying to give birth. The only people around were a couple of children about the ages of six and eight."

His hands stopped moving but continued to rest on her.

"I had the interpreter ask her if she would like me to help. Her culture dictated that she shouldn't agree but she was in so much pain she wouldn't tell me no. I had seen a baby delivered once. I'm not sure who was more scared, me or her. I sent everyone out but the interpreter. It took some explaining on the interpreter's part to get her to understand I needed to examine her. Finally she relented. The baby's shoulder was hung. I was thankful it wasn't breech, which was what I'd expected. It was work but I managed to help bring the baby into the world. It was exhilarating. The baby had a healthy cry and the mother a smile on her face when I left. Imagine living like that and still smiling. I knew then that it was far better than patching up men who had been shot or torn apart by landmines. As soon as I returned to camp I put in my papers to get out of the army."

"Did you ever see the baby again?"

"No. I never wanted to. I was afraid of what I might find. Children have a hard life in Iraq. You know, this conversation has suddenly taken a negative turn. Not what I intended. How about you tell me what you have planned for this week."

His fingers started moving over her skin again.

"I think I forgot to tell you that some of the teachers at school are giving me a shower on Monday after classes. I hope now I'll have some baby clothes to fill the drawers of the chest. I also hope to buy a few pictures for the walls. If I do, would you hang them for me?"

"As long as someone doesn't go into labor, I don't see why not."

She twisted to look at him. "Could you come out to dinner one night?"

Ryan's fingertips fluttered over her middle. "Sounds great to me. Sit up. I want to massage your lower back."

She did so and he pushed her gown up to her shoulders. He put more lotion in his hands and began to rub her lower back firmly.

"For a little bit you could get a permanent job doing that."

Ryan's hands faltered a second, then started moving again. Had she said the wrong thing?

"Well, I've done all I can to make you comfortable."

"It was wonderful. Feel free to stop by and do that anytime. If I got a foot massage and body rub on the same day, I might melt away."

"I wouldn't want you to do that. I like knowing you're around." Ryan moved out from behind her. "As much as I would enjoy staying in bed with you all day, I promised to cover for Sophia this afternoon and tomorrow until the new midwife takes over on Monday."

She hated to see this time with Ryan end.

"Mind if I get a quick shower?" he asked.

"Of course not," she said, pulling her gown back into place.

"Why don't you stay in bed, take it easy today?" Ryan suggested, as he picked up his clothes off the floor.

"Are you afraid you were too rough on me last night?"

His grin was devilish. "Are you kidding? It was

more like you being rough on me. I had no idea a pregnant woman could be so aggressive."

She threw a pillow at him. "I'll show you aggressive."

Ryan's deep laughter filled the room even after he'd closed the bathroom door behind him.

Phoebe was in the kitchen when he came in to say goodbye. His shirtsleeves were rolled halfway up his forearms. He had his jacket over his arm and his tie in his hand. A couple of damp locks of hair fell over his forehead. She had never seen anyone look more desirable.

She resisted the urge to grab his hand and beg him not to leave. When he went out the door she was afraid that fragile fairy-tale bubble they had been living in since yesterday afternoon would burst. Could she ever get it back again?

Phoebe stood with her back to the counter. "I'll be in town on Thursday for my next checkup."

"I'll see you then if not before. I have to go."

"I know. There are babies to deliver."

He grinned. "And they don't wait."

"I sure hope not. I'm ready now for this one to come." She looked at a picture on the wall instead of him, scared he might see her sadness. There had never been this type of emotion when Joshua had left and she'd known she wouldn't see him for months. She had it bad for Ryan.

Phoebe walked with him out to the veranda. At the steps he wrapped her in his arms and pulled her tightly against him, giving her a kiss. Letting her go, he hurried down the steps.

"A little overdressed for a Saturday morning, aren't you, dear?"

Phoebe smiled as Ryan threw up a hand and continued down the path. "Good morning, Mrs. Rosenheim. Beautiful day, isn't it?"

Phoebe waved as he pulled away.

"I see you found a young man who'll be around for you." Mrs. Rosenheim's voice carried across the gardens.

Phoebe waved and called, "I hope I have."

Ryan pulled up in front of his house, turned off the engine and banged his head against the steering wheel a couple of times.

What had he done? He knew the answer and didn't like it one bit. He'd spent the night with his best friend's wife. Crossed the professional line and, worse, he'd started to think of Phoebe as more than a friend. She was his lover. How low could he go?

He'd even spent most of the morning playing house with her. He had nothing emotionally to offer Phoebe. She needed someone to rely on, to love her and the baby. He wasn't that guy. He didn't commit to anybody. There wasn't even a cat or a dog in his life.

He had no intention of pledging himself to a woman with a child. Or to any woman, for that matter. He wouldn't be any good at it. Worse, didn't even want to try. He wouldn't take the chance on heartache. Fun while it lasted was all he'd ever wanted. He'd had all the pain he was willing to live with. He'd see to the practical things, like getting the baby's room ready and even delivering the baby, but then he was backing out.

Some other man would take his place. Phoebe was an attractive woman. No, that wasn't strong enough. She was beautiful and smart, funny, with a quick wit, and someone far better than him would come along. He was afraid he would hurt her, but over time she would get over it. Someone would enter her life and give her what she deserved. Maybe in time she'd forgive him.

He sat up and stared out the window. His hands tightened on the wheel. Someone else would share her bed. The thought made him sick. But it was the way things should be. For her sake and the baby's.

Ryan opened the door of the car and climbed out. There was a light mist, just as there had been the evening he'd found Phoebe on his doorstep. Would he always think of her when it rained? No, he couldn't let things go any further, but he worried they had already gone too far. He'd enjoyed her body too much, liked having someone to laugh with, eat with, to look forward to seeing. He'd never had trouble keeping himself shut off but now he couldn't seem to get past his feelings for Phoebe.

He needed to get into his shop, work. Push her out of his mind. He groaned. The project he was working on was the cradle. He wasn't even safe from her in his only sanctuary. How had she invaded his life so completely in such a short time? Why had he let her? Because he'd fallen for her.

Cared about her more than he had anyone since JT. How ironic was that?

Disgusted with himself, he climbed out of his car and slammed the door before heading for his front door.

Maybe when he finished the cradle and Phoebe delivered, he would be able to get her out of his mind. A nagging voice kept telling him that wasn't going to happen.

CHAPTER NINE

PHOEBE WALKED THROUGH the archway entrance of the hospital on Thursday afternoon on her way to her appointment. Her soft-soled shoes made squeaking sounds as she crossed the tiles on the floor of the lobby. At the lift, she pushed the button for the sixth floor. She could hardly contain her excitement over seeing Ryan.

Despite their plans, she'd not seen him since he'd left her house on Saturday morning. She'd only heard from him once. That had been a quick phone call to say that he couldn't make it to dinner. It was a full moon and he'd been busy. He needed to remain near the hospital.

She understood. When it was her turn to deliver she would want to know he was close. He had asked how she was doing but otherwise the call had been short and to the point. Still, she had to remember that he worked odd hours and had no control over when those would be.

The doors to the lift whooshed open and she entered. Would he kiss her? Probably not. That would be very unprofessional during an antenatal visit. Maybe he would take her out to eat or, better yet, home. She had missed his touch but more than that she missed talking and laughing with him.

She was acting like a silly schoolgirl with her first crush. Here she was almost a mother and giddy over a man.

The lift doors opened again and Phoebe stepped out and walked toward the clinic. Inside, she signed in at the window. She took a chair and looked at the pictures of the medical staff lining the wall. They included Ryan. He looked handsome but far too serious in his picture. Nothing like the man with the good sense of humor that she knew. Besides him there were a number of people she'd met or recognized from the wedding.

"Phoebe."

It was Ryan's voice. She would have known it anywhere. Every night she heard it in her dreams. Her head jerked up and their gazes met. There was a flicker of delight in his before it turned guarded. Wasn't he glad to see her?

Phoebe smiled. "Hi."

He cleared his throat and said, "Hello. Are you ready to come back?"

She moved to stand. It took her a second more than she would have liked but Ryan hadn't moved from his position at the door. A few days ago he would have hurried to offer her help. "Yes, I'm ready."

"Come this way."

What was going on? Maybe he didn't want anyone to see him touch her or overhear them. Still, this was a little much. She'd always spoken in a friendly manner to Sophia. That was part of the appeal of having a midwife—it was more like having a friend there to help deliver her.

"Follow me," he said, and led her down the hallway to an exam room. Once she'd entered he closed the door.

She sat on the exam table.

"So how have you been?" Ryan asked, as if speaking to someone he'd just met.

Phoebe gave him a questioning look. Ryan couldn't see it because his focus was on the computer. Other than those few seconds when their eyes had met after he'd called her name he hadn't looked at her again.

"Any pains?"

Just in her heart all of a sudden. "No."

"Well, it won't be long now."

Why was he talking to her like that? As if he didn't really know her? Was he afraid someone might walk in on them? "No, it won't. Next week is my due date."

He finally looked up but his focus was over her right shoulder. "You know that the chance of a baby coming on a due date is slim. A first baby is almost always late."

"I know." This all business attitude was getting old. "How are you, Ryan? I've missed you this week."

He went back to studying the computer screen. "I've been busy. Sophia being out makes things a little complicated."

Apparently their relationship was included in that.

"Any chance we could get something to eat this evening?"

"I have a mother in labor on her way in. I'm going to the unit as soon as I'm finished here."

Phoebe had never received the brush-off before but she recognized it when she heard it. *I won't cry, I won't cry.* She clenched her teeth.

Ryan was acting as if they'd never been intimate. But they were at the clinic and he should act professionally. But he was overdoing it.

He left without giving her another look.

What had happened between now and Saturday morning that had made him so distant? He was acting like the guy she'd met that first night. When he returned she was going to find out what was going on.

She was prepared and waiting on the table when he returned. He wasn't by himself. A woman in her midtwenties followed him into the room.

"Phoebe, this is Stacy. She's the new midwife who has joined our group. Would you be willing to let her do the exam?"

She looked at him in disbelief. He wouldn't meet her gaze. Now he didn't even want to touch her.

"All right." Phoebe drew the words out.

Stacy stepped to the table. "Phoebe, may I

check the position of the baby? I promise I have gentle hands."

Phoebe said nothing. She knew gentle hands and those belonged to Ryan.

As Stacy's hand moved over her expanded middle, she rattled off some numbers while Ryan typed on the computer.

"Well, you're doing fine. Everything is as it should be. I don't see why you won't have an uneventful delivery," Stacy gushed. "I look forward to being there."

"What?" Phoebe looked at Ryan. Nothing was as it should be.

He looked over her head as he spoke. "Stacy is going to step in for me. My, uh, caseload is heavy and she's taking some of my patients."

Stacy was all smiles when she said, "I'll see you here next week for your appointment or at the delivery, whichever comes first. Do you have any questions for us?"

Yes, she had a pile of questions but none that she could ask in front of Stacy.

"No" came out sounding weak.

"Okay, then. I'll see you next week," Stacy said,

without seeming to notice the tension between her and Ryan.

He opened the door and left without even looking at her. Stacy followed.

Phoebe sat in silence. Stunned. Never had she felt so used. She'd shared her body with Ryan. Opened her heart. Believed that she meant something to him. Now he was treating her like she was nothing. What a jerk. He didn't even have the backbone to tell her that he no longer wanted to help deliver the baby.

She climbed off the table and dressed. Had she ever felt more humiliated? Discarded?

Ryan was there four hours later when a new life entered the world. This time he missed the amazement he usually felt. All he could think about was Phoebe's large sad eyes when he'd left the exam room. What must she think of him? Probably the same as he was thinking of himself.

He had called to check on her a few days earlier, using all his self-control to wait as long as he had before he'd picked up the phone. Justifying the call, he'd told himself he was after all her midwife. But that hadn't been the real reason he'd done it. He'd been desperate to hear her voice. He'd done some difficult things in his life but acting as if he didn't care about Phoebe in front of her had been the hardest. It had been even more challenging not to touch her. She'd looked so dejected when he'd walked out of the room. The devil of it all was that he cared about Phoebe more than anyone else in the world.

The irony was that he had treated her the way he had because he couldn't deal with the depth of his feelings for her and his inability to handle the mountain of guilt for how he had treated someone who had been important to JT. He was so messed up he had no business being involved with anyone. Until Phoebe, he had managed to keep everyone at bay, but she had slipped past his defenses.

The dark of the night mirrored his emotions as he drove home hours later. For once in his life he wished someone was there to come home to. He let himself into his house and dropped his clothes on the floor. That was a habit that he and Phoebe shared. They both dropped things as soon as they came in the door. He his clothes and she her shoes.

Going to his bedroom, he flipped on the light. When he looked at his bed all he could see was the way Phoebe had lovingly admired his work. He'd never shared his workshop with anyone before. Even the few times female company had stayed over he'd never taken them down there. It had taken one sunny day of driving Phoebe around to garage sales to open it to her.

How quickly she had found a way into his home, his shop and his heart. But none of that mattered. He would never be able to be there for her as she needed. She deserved someone who could open his heart completely. Hold nothing back. Be there for her for the long haul. He wouldn't invest in people that way after he had he'd lost so many of them. He couldn't take the chance of going there again. It was better to let her go now.

Ryan turned off the light, removed his clothes but didn't bother to pull the covers back before he lay on the bed. He squeezed his eyes shut and put his arm over his eyes. All he could see was the confusion, then disappointment and pain in Phoebe's eyes.

Had he ever been happier than he had been in

the last few weeks? When had he last thought about even being happy? It certainly hadn't been for a long time. He could remember that emotion. A few times when he'd been a kid. But he'd recognized happiness when Phoebe had kissed him on the cheek. Or when they had watched the little penguins waddle out of the water to take care of their chicks, or the look on Phoebe's face when she'd looked down at him as they'd become one. Because of her he'd known true happiness.

He hadn't realized how he'd shut out the world until she had shown up on his doorstep, leaving him no choice but to rejoin it again. He'd carried the pain of war, the agony of trying to help men and women whose lives would never be the same, bottled up until Phoebe had started asking questions. He'd talked more about his time in the war in the last few weeks than he'd done in the last ten years. The more he'd told her the easier it had become to talk about those times. Now it felt like a weight had been lifted off his chest. After he'd returned from a difficult mission, he'd been required to talk to the shrink. He'd never thought it useful. Thanks to Phoebe, he was starting to see a value in not holding those memories in.

All this didn't matter anyway. He'd hurt Phoebe so badly today that even if he tried to have a relationship with her she would close the door in his face. No, it was better this way.

Phoebe leaned her head against the glass window of the tram. The clack of the cars made a rhythm that would have lulled her to sleep if her emotions hadn't been jumping like balls in a pinball machine. She fluctuated between disbelief and anger.

How had she let Ryan matter so much? Worse, how had she been misled by him?

He had made her believe he cared. It hadn't only been his lovemaking but the way he'd thought of little things to help her. Painting the baby's room, going with her to garage sales, massaging her feet. Her back. In just a few weeks he had done more for her and with her than Joshua had done during their entire marriage.

So what had happened to make Ryan do such an about-face?

Had she pushed too hard? Assumed things she shouldn't? Had making plans for them to eat together, see each other scared him off?

When she heard her stop called she prepared to get off. She still had a few blocks to walk before she made it home. She was tired. Didn't even plan to eat anything before going to bed. If Ryan knew he would scold her. Maybe not, after what she'd experienced today.

Slipping her key into the lock a few minutes later, she opened the door. She entered and turned on the light. How different this homecoming had been from the one she had imagined. She'd hoped that Ryan would bring her home and stay the night. That bubble had been completely popped.

Phoebe kicked her shoes off. She chuckled dryly. The action made her think of Ryan dropping his clothes inside his door. Making her way to her bedroom, she turned on her bedside lamp, then undressed. She slid between the sheets and leaned over to turn the light off. The picture of her and Joshua caught her attention.

Had the fact that she was carrying Joshua's baby been the reason Ryan had suddenly slammed the door between them? Was the baby too much of a reminder that she would always be tied to Joshua? Or was it that they represented the painful loss of Joshua? Or the other men that Ryan had seen die. In some way they must be part of the past he worked so hard to shut out or forget.

Sliding the drawer out of the bedside table, Phoebe pulled out the crumpled letter Joshua had sent her. Opening it, she smoothed it out on the bed before reading it. Had Joshua known he wasn't coming home when he had written it? Had he known he was leaving on a dangerous patrol like Ryan had described? Even after they had discussed separating, had he wanted her to be happy, to find someone else? Had he thought Ryan might be that person?

Whatever it was, she'd done as Joshua had said and gone to Ryan. Joshua had been right. There she'd found the piece of her life that had been missing all these years. Moisture filled her eyes. But Ryan didn't want her. Once again she was on her own. Would she ever find a real partner in life?

Turning off the light, she curled around her baby. At least this little one would be someone to love who would return it.

Sunday afternoon there was a knock at the door.

Her heart leaped. Was it Ryan?

Phoebe answered it to find Mrs. Rosenheim waiting on the veranda. Phoebe's spirits dropped like a person falling off a bridge. Had she really expected it to be Ryan?

"Hello, dear. I was just checking on you. I've not seen you all weekend. Didn't want you to have that baby and me not know about it."

"I'm right here. No baby yet." She didn't want any company. How could she get rid of her neighbor gracefully?

"From the sound and look of you, something else is going on." Mrs. Rosenheim brushed past Phoebe into the living room.

Phoebe really didn't feel up to dealing with the older woman. She wanted to wallow in her misery alone.

"I haven't seen that nice young man around."

That was all it took for Phoebe to burst into tears.

"My goodness, it's all that bad?" Mrs. Rosenheim patted her on the arm. "Why don't you fix us some tea and tell me all about it?"

Phoebe swiped at her cheek, then nodded. Maybe it would be good to tell someone about what had happened.

As she put the kettle on and prepared the cups, Phoebe told Mrs. Rosenheim about how she'd met Ryan.

"Well, at least that absent husband of yours did one thing to show he cared," Mrs. Rosenheim murmured.

"Joshua cared—"

Mrs. Rosenheim waved her hand. "Let's not argue about that. So, what put you in this tizzy about Ryan?"

Phoebe placed a teacup in front of Mrs. Rosenheim and one in front of the chair across from her. She wouldn't sit in Ryan's chair. How quickly he had become a central part of her life.

Phoebe told her about how Ryan had acted during her clinic visit. During the entire explanation Mrs. Rosenheim sipped her tea and nodded.

"Sounds scared to me. So what do you plan to do?"

"Do? What can I do?"

"Yes, do. You're getting ready to have a baby. Do you want to bring a baby into the world feeling that kind of discord? Go and make Ryan explain himself. Tell him how you feel."

Phoebe sighed. "You're right. I need to talk

him. Get the air cleared. I was so shocked and hurt by his actions that I've not been able to think."

"Then I suggest that you make yourself presentable and give that man a piece of your mind."

Ryan already had her heart, he might as well get part of her mind. If things stayed the way they were, she would lose him. To move on she needed answers, and those could only come from Ryan.

Phoebe bowed her head against the wind that was picking up as she walked along Ryan's street. Like the first time she had visited him, she had practiced what she was going to say on the tram ride there. She was going to demand answers. More than that, she was going to get answers.

Would Ryan be home? She'd thought of calling first but had been afraid that he would make some excuse as to why she couldn't see him. She would have none of that.

She had accepted Joshua's decisions. Knowing what he did was important hadn't disguised the fact he'd been more interested in fighting wars than being with her. She wouldn't let Ryan put her to the side. She'd stay at his place until she knew what was going on.

Phoebe walked past Ryan's car. He was home. She climbed the steps to his door and groaned. Her back was killing her. The baby had grown so large.

She hesitated. Would Ryan answer if he realized it was her? It didn't matter. She was staying until she found out what his problem was, even if she had to sleep on his veranda all night. That wouldn't happen. No matter how hard Ryan was trying to push her out of his life, he was too kind and tenderhearted to leave her out in the elements.

To come all this way and not knock was ridiculous. She was no longer the woman she'd been when she'd shown up on his doorstep last month. With or without him, she would have this baby and the two of them would make it. It would be wonderful to have Ryan in their lives, but if not, she and the baby would still survive. That much she did know.

Lifting her hand, she boldly knocked on the door. Seconds went by with no answer. There was no sound from inside. Again she knocked.

Nothing. Maybe Ryan was in the basement and couldn't hear her. She turned to descend the steps and search for a way around back when the door opened.

Ryan looked as if he hadn't slept in days. There were dark circles under his eyes. His hair stood on end. He was still wearing his hospital uniform and it was rumpled, as if he'd been too distracted to change. Her heart went out to him for a second and then she reminded herself of why she was there. Life hadn't been kind to her since last Thursday, either.

CHAPTER TEN

PHOEBE.

Ryan's heart skidded to a halt then picked up the pace double-time. What was she doing here?

How like her to show up unannounced on his doorstep. Was that how they had started out?

She looked wonderful, irritated and determined all at the same time. He had missed her. There had never been another time in his life when he'd longed for someone like he had for Phoebe.

"What're are you doing here?"

"We need to talk." She stepped forward, leaving him no choice but to move and let her in.

"Talk?"

She whirled to face him with surprising agility. "You mean after your performance the other day you don't think we need to talk?"

Ryan closed the door. He really didn't want to do this. "Performance?"

"Really, Ryan? You don't think you owe me an explanation for your behavior at the clinic?"

"I did my job."

"Job? Was it your job to take pity on the poor widow woman and go to bed with her?"

Ryan flinched. That hurt. Yes, she was hitting below the belt but he deserved it.

"What I don't understand is why I let you get away with acting like there was nothing between us. Or why I've given you so many days to explain yourself. I didn't expect a public display at the clinic but I did expect you to act as if I had some importance."

"Stacy was there—"

"That's your excuse for going AWOL on me and not hearing from you? You know, I would never have taken you for a coward."

Ryan winced. That's what he had been. If he ran, then he wouldn't have to face what he'd done and how he felt about Phoebe. He sat in his chair. Phoebe's glare bore down on him. "Look, you don't understand."

"Oh, I understand. This is all about you hiding from the world, the things you saw in Iraq and your feelings. If you don't let someone in, then you don't have to worry about them dying, like your friends did. Like Joshua.

"You live mechanically. You just go through the days. Look at this place." She swung her arm around, indicating the room. "You just exist here. No pictures, no rugs, a sofa and a chair. Your bedroom is a step better only because of your woodwork. It shows some warmth. The one place where you actually look like you're living is ironically in your shop, and it's underground. You come up and do what you have to do and then disappear again like a mole that's afraid of the light, but in your case you're afraid of feeling anything for someone. You care more about that furniture downstairs than you do people. In fact, those inanimate objects in your bedroom have received more love than you show the rest of the people in your life."

She was right. There was nothing he could say to defend himself.

"You're afraid that if you care too much you'll lose part of yourself. But you'll never be happy that way. You have to let people in. Let them see the person I see. The warm and caring person. The fun and humorous one. The person who gives despite any pain to himself."

Ryan raised a hand with his index finger up. "Hey, don't be putting me on a pedestal. I'm not one of your fairy-tale knights on a white horse, riding in to save the day."

Phoebe looked at him. Was he right? Had she tried to make more of their relationship than there was? Had she been so desperate that she had clung to Ryan? Needed anyone to rely on? To fill the void of loneliness?

"I haven't." Her remark sounded weak even to her own ears.

"Haven't what? Become self-contained, built your own perfect little world where Joshua came home as the hero, loved you and left to return again? Where you were willing to accept a small piece of his life just so you could have someone to share that perfect life? Except it wasn't all that perfect, was it? You wanted more. A family, but you couldn't or wouldn't tell him that it was time to think of you."

She cringed. Was that what she had been doing? "You're wrong."

"Really? Did you ever once ask JT to take an assignment that would bring him home for longer than three months? Did you ever ask him to choose you over the army?"

She hadn't.

"I can see you didn't. What were you afraid of? That he would leave you all together? As strong as you act on the outside, you're a marshmallow of self-doubt on the inside. You don't understand why you weren't good enough to make JT want to stay at home. You feel sorry for yourself but cover it with acting as if you can handle everything on your own. No matter how hard I might try, I could never fix those for you. That's something you have to recognize and do for yourself."

All Ryan's accusations hit home. A number of them she didn't want to face.

"Phoebe, I can't be someone that I'm not. Seeing what humans can do to each other makes you stop and think before you get involved. I cared then and what did it get me? All I wanted was out." He spoke to the floor, then looked at her.

"That's understandable. But look at you now." She lowered her voice. "You help bring life into the world. You sure picked a funny occupation to not care about anyone."

"That was part of the appeal of being a midwife. I'm only involved in a patient's life for a short time. After the baby comes I'm done."

"How sad. You know you brought warmth and joy into my world. I came to your doorstep lonely, sad and afraid. For heaven's sake, I was weeks away from having a baby and I didn't even have a room ready. I was going through the motions, just like you, until we met. It was far past time for us both to start living our lives again."

"I have lived like that. I've had friends. Joshua was a friend and look what happened to him. You say that I'm afraid but you are afraid of something, too, and that is being alone. You've lost your parents, you brother is nowhere around, Joshua is gone, his parents are jerks and now you're clinging to me. People leave and die, it's a part of life."

Phoebe stepped forward. "I'm well aware of that. The question is, are you? People die. Do you think I don't understand that? He was my husband. My parents are gone. Even my brother is halfway across the world from me."

Ryan jumped up. Phoebe stepped backward. He move forward and glared at her. With his hands balled at his sides, he barked, "And I'm the man who slept with his best friend's wife."

Phoebe blinked and stumbled backwards. She quickly righted herself. That was what all of this was about? Some male idea of solidarity to his best friend. Ryan thought he'd betrayed Joshua.

He made a sound of disgust and turned away. His shoulders were tense. She wanted to reach out and touch him. Reassure him that he'd done nothing wrong. If she did, she feared he'd reject her forever. She had to reason with him, get through to him. Reaching into her pocket, she pulled out Joshua's letter. Maybe with Joshua's help she could.

"Ryan, Joshua is dead."

He jerked slightly.

"We're alive." She kept her voice low. "He doesn't stand between us. He's gone. You did nothing wrong. In fact, it was very right. Here, I think you should read this." She stepped around him and handed him the letter. "I'm going to leave you to read it."

Walking to the bedroom, she went into the bathroom. Her back was aching. Maybe the baby was just pressing against something it shouldn't. Would Joshua's letter help Ryan let go or would it only make things worse? She hoped with all her heart it made him see the truth.

Ryan opened the crumpled pages. Why had Phoebe given him something to read? He scanned the page and saw JT's name at the end. Guilt churned in his stomach. With his heart bumping against his chest wall and his hands shaking, he let his focus move to the top of the page.

Phoebe—

I know I've not always written like I should. For that I'm sorry. Especially when you have been so good about it. I know now that when we married you didn't bargain on us spending so much time apart. For that I'm sorry also. When we parted a few weeks ago I knew things had changed between us. We have spent too much time living separate lives to the point where our relationship has slipped into one of friendship instead of one that we both wish it could be. I have done you an injustice. You have such a large capacity to love that it was never fair of me to deny you that.

I wish for you a happy life. If you ever need anything and don't know where to turn I want you to find my friend, Ryan Matthews. He will help you. We are buddies from his army days. I trust him with my life and you can with yours. He lives in Melbourne. He will take care of you. Believe in him, he won't let you down. I think you will like him. I hope you do.

Take care, Phoebe. Have a good life.

Joshua

JT had sent Phoebe to him. As if he'd known they would needed each other. Had it been JT's way of giving his blessing to their relationship? He looked at the letter. How long had Phoebe had this? Why hadn't she said something sooner?

Ryan went into his room. Phoebe must have purposely taken her time in the bathroom because she was coming toward him. She stopped and stared at the cradle sitting in a corner. She must have missed it on her way to the bathroom because the closet door stood open, obscuring it.

It was his finest piece of work to date. He didn't know if he would ever do better. It was as if his heart and soul had been emptied into it. It sat low to the floor with a high front and sides that wrapped around slightly. It looked like one that would be handed down in a wealthy family. It was as much like one he'd seen in a history museum back home as he could make it.

Going over to the cradle, Phoebe ran her hand along the smooth lip of one side. She pushed it and watched the slow movement back and forth.

"It's for the baby." The emotion in his voice made it come out as a croak.

She glanced at him. "It's the most beautiful thing I've ever seen."

He raised his hand with Joshua's letter in it. "This is why you came here that first night."

She nodded.

"Why didn't you tell me?"

"At first because you acted all cold and unwelcoming and I wasn't sure Joshua had been right about you."

His lips formed a tight line. "I wasn't at my best. I'm sorry. So why not later?"

She shrugged. "I started to trust you. You agreed to deliver the baby. I wanted you to and the letter didn't matter anymore. I had started to care about you. I had hoped you cared about me. Thought you did until I saw you on Thursday."

"I'm sorry I hurt you. I hated doing so but I didn't know how else to handle it. The night we made love was the most wonderful of my life but on my way home I thought of Joshua, of how I was not the best man for you. I knew we couldn't continue." He looked at the letter. "But after reading his letter, I wonder..."

"If it was Joshua's way of telling us both to move on? That we would need each other? I don't know if he thought this..." she pointed to him and then herself "...would happen, but I think he knew we could help each other. We were the two people he knew best in the world. I don't think what's between us is wrong. I think we honor him by caring about each other and living well.

I love you, Ryan, and want you in my and this baby's life. By the way, you could have talked to me on Thursday, just like you are doing now."

His chest tightened. He'd rather die than not be the person Phoebe needed him to be. "I don't know if I can give what you and the baby should have."

Her look met his. "I don't think either one of us knows that for sure. Yes, there're risks but that's what love is all about. Think with your heart, not your head. I know you care." She touched her chest. "I feel it here. That was part of the reason I came." She grinned. "And because I was so mad. But everything you do proves you care. For example…" she touched the cradle "…you messed up with this. It shows your true feelings. You care. There's no doubt that you do, you're just scared of doing so.

"I've been waiting most of my life to have someone love me, really love me, want to be with me. I thought it was Joshua but I soon learned we didn't want the same things. I wanted the rocker on the veranda and watching the sunset and he wanted to always be going off somewhere. Don't get me wrong, what he was doing was important but that didn't bring me any closer to my dreams.

"I love you, Ryan. I don't want you doing anything for me out of obligation to Joshua any more. I want you to care about me for me."

Could he be a part of that? He wasn't sure. But he had been for the last six weeks. He'd never been happier. Had he found the place he belonged? The place where all the ugliness in life disappeared? When had the last time been he'd thought of the war? He'd already realized that talking to Phoebe had eased the past. Now, could he grasp what she was offering and hang on to it?

There was a silence between them. The air between them was heavy with tension.

"I guess I should be going."

She sounded defeated.

"I've said what I came to say. Found out what I needed to know." She moved past him and headed for the door.

Fear flooded him that surpassed any he'd ever felt before. Even when bullets had been flying over his head. If he let her go out the door he might lose her forever. He couldn't let that happen. His fingers wrapped around her forearm, stopping her.

Her gaze came up to meet his. There was a question there, along with hope.

"I don't want you to leave."

Her hand came up to cup his cheek. "I don't want to go."

The band around his chest popped, letting all the love he'd held back flow. He gathered her to him and brought his mouth to hers. Phoebe melted against him. Deep kisses, small sweet ones, filled his world until they broke apart.

"Can you stay the night?" Ryan looked down at her.

"Yes. My maternity leave starts tomorrow. No due babies?"

"Only this one." Ryan placed his hand on her belly. "And I intend to keep a close eye on him or her. Not let the mother out of my sight or out of my arms."

Phoebe smiled, one that reached her eyes. "That sounds perfect to me. I promise to be willing to accept life isn't about fairy tales if you're willing to believe they are a possibility."

"Agreed." Ryan kissed her again.

She broke away. "Augh." She reached behind her and rubbed her lower back.

"What's wrong?"

"My back aches."

He gave her an intense look. "When did it start?"

"On my way here."

He grinned. "You may be in labor."

"Really?" Her hands went to her belly and a dreamy look covered her face.

"We'll see what happens in the next few hours. It still might be Braxton-Hicks contractions or, in other words, false labor pains. Come with me. I have something we can do to keep your mind off them." He took her hand and led her toward the bath.

"Can we do that if I'm in labor?"

Ryan chuckled. "No, but there are plenty of other things that we can do that are almost as satisfying."

"Like a foot massage?"

"That could be arranged. But I have some new

ideas in mind. Like starting with a nice warm shower."

Inside the bathroom, he reached in the tub area. Turning the water on, seconds later the shower sprayed water. Ryan turned back to her and began removing her clothes.

"I can do that."

"But I want to." He carefully worked each button out of its hole. Soon she was naked. He didn't touch her but he took his time looking.

"You're embarrassing me."

"Because I enjoy admiring you? I think you're the most amazing woman I know." With a look of regret he pulled the curtain back and offered her his hand. "Be careful. We don't need you slipping."

Phoebe took it and stepped under the steaming water. A few minutes later the curtain was pulled back and Ryan joined her. His manhood stood tall between them. He was dazzling. "Oh, I wasn't expecting you."

"I need a bath, too. Saves water to share. Turn around and let me massage your back."

Phoebe did as he instructed. He made slow circles with the pads of his thumbs pressing but not too hard.

"That feels great."

Ryan continued to ease the ache for a few more minutes before his hands moved around to make wide circular motions over her belly. He pulled her back against him. His length pressed against her butt. He didn't move but said close to her ear, "Hand me the soap."

She took it out of the holder and placed it in his hand. He stepped back and began to run the soap across her shoulders, then down her back. "Turn around."

Phoebe did. His hands traveled to her breasts. She watched the tension grow in his face. A muscle jumped in his jaw. He continued his ministrations. Her nipples grew and tingled. His hand moved on to her belly and down to do her legs. As he stood he kissed the baby.

Her breath caught and her lips quivered. She put her hands on both sides of Ryan's face and brought his mouth to hers. He returned her kiss, then set her away.

"You need to get out before the water turns cold."

"What about you?"

"I think I'll stay for a while."

Phoebe stepped out of the shower with a smile on her face. It was nice, being desired. She dried off. "Ryan, I don't have any more clothes. Do you have a large shirt I can wear?"

"You don't need any clothes. Just climb into bed. Is your back still hurting?"

"A little. It comes and goes."

A few minutes later Ryan came out of the bathroom in all his naked glory. He was all man. Leaving the room, he returned with a fat candle and a pack of matches. He set the candle on the bedside table and lit it before he turned off the overhead light.

"Move over." He climbed in next to her. "Face me, Phoebe."

She rolled to her side and he did also. Ryan's hand started rubbing her belly and moving around to her back and forward again. He looked into her eyes.

A few minutes later he cleared his throat. "I

loved the aggressive way you pushed your way in here tonight and made me see reason. JT and I could have used you on patrol with us a couple of times."

She snickered. "I actually learned that maneuver from Mrs. Rosenheim. She's been using it on me for a few years now. In fact, she did so this afternoon. She's the one who encouraged me to come and see you."

"Well, remind me to give her a kiss when I see her again."

Phoebe placed her hand on his chest. "You might not want to do that because she could expect it every time you see her."

"I think it'll be worth taking the chance." He captured her hand and held it against him.

"Ryan, I want you to know that I'm not going to push you for more than you can give or do. Ooh…" Phoebe tensed.

He looked at her closely. "Stronger?"

"A little."

"Why don't you try to get some sleep? You may need it later. I'll be right here." Ryan rolled to his back and pulled her closer. His length lay firm against her hip. Regardless of his obvious need, he made no move to do anything but care for her. She drifted off to sleep knowing she and the baby were in good hands. A sharp pain radiating around her waist woke her. The candle had burned low.

"How're you doing?"

"That pain was stronger."

Ryan set up in bed. "Then we need to start timing them. Let me know when you feel the next one."

She lifted one corner of her mouth and gave him a look. "I don't think you'll have to be told. I'm a wimp when it comes to pain. You'll hear me."

He chuckled. "I'll keep that in mind as this goes on. Do I need to call in someone else so they can lose their hearing?"

"You've already done that with Stacy."

Ryan had the good grace to look repentant. "I'm sorry about that. I'll try to make up for that by doing what I can to help make you comfortable. Do you need anything? Need more support on your back?"

"I'm fine right now but I do love to have my back rubbed."

"Then a back rub is what you'll get." He climbed out of bed.

"Where're you going?"

"I'm just going around to the other side."

"But I liked you here." She watched him walk by the end of the bed. Even in labor he turned her on.

"I appreciate the compliment but I can do a better job over here. Less distractions." His hands moved across her back.

"Like what?"

"Your beautiful face. When your pains get to twenty minutes apart we'll need to call Stacy and go to the hospital."

"Do we have to? I want you to deliver," she said in a melancholy tone.

"No, I guess we don't have to. Do you want to deliver at your house? If you do, we need to get moving."

"I'd like to have the baby here. In this beautiful bed. Just you and me."

Did he realize that if he agreed it would be a

sign of commitment? He was giving her and the baby permission to enter his personal space. To share his home and bed for a significant event.

Ryan's hands stopped moving for a second then started again. "I would like that."

She smiled, then winced.

"I take it that was another pain. Try to breathe through them. It'll make it easier. Remember your lessons."

"Is this the moment that you morph into a midwife?"

"It's time. I'm going to get my bag and put on some pants. You stay put."

"You're going to put on clothes when I'm not wearing any?"

"It's a long shot that something might go wrong. If I have to call for help I don't want to get caught with my pants down, so to speak."

Phoebe laughed.

He gave her a reprimanding look. "You go on and make fun but it would be hard for me to live that one down."

She enjoyed the sight of Ryan's backside as he search a drawer. He pulled out some boxers and stepped into them. Going to the wardrobe, he came out wearing a pair of athletic shorts. He then left the room and returned with a backpack. Ryan flipped the bedside lamp on and blew out the candle.

"I liked it better the other way." Phoebe rolled toward him.

"I did, too, but I need to see." Ryan unzipped the backpack and removed a stethoscope. He placed it on her belly, then listened to her chest and back. Finished, he put the stethoscope on the table. "Sounds good."

"I'm scared" slipped out before she knew it.

Ryan pushed her hair away from her forehead and kissed her. "There's nothing to be afraid of. I'll be right here with you all the way. This is a natural process."

"That's coming from a man who never had a baby."

"That's true, but I've been there when a lot of them have been born. I'll give you an example of how natural it is. My great-great-grandmother had twelve babies. They all lived. While she was in labor she would fix breakfast for the family and get everyone off to the fields. They were farmers in north Alabama. She would lie on the floor and have the baby, then tie the cord off with a thread from a flour sack because it was thin enough to cut the cord. She would clean herself and the baby up, then get into bed. At the end of the day when everyone came in from the field there would be a new baby to greet."

"Are you expecting me to do that?" Her voice rose.

Ryan took her hand and squeezed it. "No, I'm not. What I'm trying to say is that if my grandmother can do it by herself twelve times, then the two of us can certainly do it together once without any problem."

"I think I can do anything as long as I have you to help me."

Ryan leaned over and gave her a leisurely kiss. "I feel the same way, honey."

Another pain gripped her. She clutched Ryan's hand.

When it had passed he said, "Why don't you walk around some? It would help with the pain and get the labor moving along."

"I'm not going to walk around your place with no clothes on, in labor or not."

"Okay, let me see if I can find something comfortable for you to wear." Ryan went to his wardrobe. The sound of hangers being pushed across a rod came out of the space. "This should do it."

He returned to the bed with a button-up shirt in his hand. "Swing your feet over the side and I'll help you get this on."

She did and he held the shirt while she slipped her arms into it. The sleeves fell well past her hands. Ryan buttoned it for her, then rolled the sleeves up to the middle of her forearms.

He reached out and wiggled his fingers. "Let me help you stand."

Phoebe took them and let him pull her to her feet.

Ryan stepped back and looked at her. "Cute. I do believe I like you wearing my shirt."

Phoebe pushed at her hair, trying to bring it to some kind of order. "Thanks. I just hope I don't mess it up."

"Not a problem. It'll be for a good cause.

"Okay, let's do some walking. There isn't as

much space here as there is at the hospital but we'll just make do."

Ryan stayed by her side as they made a pass round the living room through the kitchen and back to the bedroom. "Let's do it again," he encouraged as she looked wistfully at the bed. With each contraction Ryan checked his watch, which he had slipped on his wrist before they'd started out of his bedroom.

"They're getting closer."

After one particularly lengthy pain he said, "Tell me about your shower at school."

It was his sly way of keeping her mind off what was going on with her body. She was grateful for his efforts. "It was wonderful. I received all kinds of cute baby things."

He touched her arm to encourage her to keep walking. "Did you get some baby clothes, like you were hoping?"

"I did. I filled a drawer and have some hanging in the wardrobe."

"You must have had a lot of people there."

They continued the slow pace around the house. "I was surprised. Most of the teachers came.

Those who didn't sent presents by others. Everyone was very generous."

"Why were you surprised? Haven't you been working there for some time?"

"I have but they have all seemed to be a little standoffish since Joshua was killed. It became worse when I told them I was pregnant. It was as if they didn't know what to say or do so they did nothing."

"I'm sorry you were so alone for so long. You should have come to me sooner."

She stopped and looked at him.

He put up a hand. "I know, I know. I wasn't very approachable at first. For that I'm sorry."

She smiled. "But you came around very nicely, so I'm happy." But he hadn't said anything about loving her. Even when she had confessed her love for him. She could wait. Ryan showed he cared in so many other ways. He was someone she could count on. Even if she couldn't, she had learned she could depend on herself. "Oh."

"Breathe. Don't hold your breath." Ryan showed her how.

They made small swooshing sounds together.

"I think it's time to get you settled in. I also need to check and see where that baby is."

Ryan led her toward the bedroom.

"How much longer?" As she went by the footboard, she let her fingers trail over the surface of the wood.

"Let me examine you, then I'll have an idea."

She sat on the edge of the bed while he prepared it.

"You're not going to make me lie on the floor like your great-great-grandmother did?"

"I hadn't planned to, but I can." He shook out a blanket as if getting ready to place it on the floor.

"I was kidding."

He smiled. "I'm glad to hear that. I was worried about my back hurting when I bent over to help deliver."

"What kind of midwife are you? Being more worried about your comfort than mine?"

Ryan put a hand down on the mattress on each side of her. His face was inches away from hers. "Honey, I care too much about you to let you be uncomfortable." Ryan kissed her deeply and moved away. He helped her settle into the center of the bed and then he did the exam.

"You're well on your way. Dilated five centimeters. When you get to ten you'll be ready to have a baby."

Another pain cramped her back and radiated around to her sides. She grabbed Ryan's hand. He rode it out with her, all the time whispering sweet encouragement.

Ryan had seen countless husbands in the delivery suite when their wives had been giving birth. Some handled the process with aplomb while others were just a step above worthless. Ryan knew what was going to happen and still waves the size of a tsunami rolled through his stomach because this time it was Phoebe having the baby and he was that significant other helping. He felt more like that guy who was useless.

She had taken over his life, captured his heart and made him a ball of nerves in a situation where he usually had all the confidence. Even with all his reassurances, he worried that something might not go right during the birth. If she died or the baby did, he didn't know what he would do. He'd survived other deaths but he didn't think he could live without Phoebe.

"You look worried all of a sudden. Is something wrong?" Phoebe asked.

"No, everything is fine. You're doing wonderfully. Keep up the good work."

"I need to go to the bathroom?"

"Sure." Ryan stood and helped her up. "I'll leave the door open. If you need me I'll be right out here."

While Phoebe was in the bathroom Ryan pulled out his cellphone and called the hospital to let them know that he was in the process of delivering Phoebe's baby. He wanted them aware so that if there was a problem someone could be here to help in minutes.

"Ryan!"

"Yes?" He hurried toward the bathroom.

"My waters just broke."

"Well, this baby is getting ready to make a showing. Stay put and I'll help you get cleaned up. I'll find you something dry to wear."

He left to search for another shirt. This time

he went to the chest of drawers and found a T-shirt. It might not fit over all of her middle but at least it would cover her lovely breasts so that he could concentrate on delivering the baby. He went back to Phoebe.

"You're going to run out of clothes." She pushed a button through a hole.

"If I do, I won't mind. I like you better naked anyway."

Moisture filled her eyes and she gave him a wry smile. "Thanks. You really are being wonderful."

"Not a problem." A delivery had always been a matter-of-fact event for him. A job with a happy ending most of the time. But with Phoebe it was much more. This was an event to cherish.

He helped her pull the T-shirt over her head.

"This doesn't cover much," she complained.

"I need to see your belly and you can pull the sheet up to cover yourself if you must. I don't know why you're being so modest. I've seen all of you and there isn't anything or anyone more stunning. Now, come on and get into bed. We have a baby to welcome into the world."

Another pain shot through her.

"Let's get you settled and I'm going to have another look." He help her move to the center of the bed.

"I'm feeling pressure."

"Good, then you're almost ready. Bend your legs."

Ryan placed her feet in the correct spot so he could see. He put on plastic gloves and checked her. "You're almost there."

"Here comes another one." Phoebe gritted her teeth.

"Look at me," Ryan demanded.

She did.

"Now, let's breathe together."

Phoebe followed his lead.

With the contraction over, Ryan lightly trailed his fingers over her middle until the tension left her and she lay back.

"I need to get a few things out of the bathroom and find something soft to swaddle the baby in. You should have let me know you were planning this tonight and I could have been better prepared."

"You're a funny man, Ryan Matthews."

"I thought you could use some humor right about now." He found the things he needed and placed them at the foot of the bed within arm's length.

Another pain took Phoebe and she met his look. They went through it together. This was one time he didn't mind looking into the pain in someone's eyes.

"I feel pressure. I need to push."

"Hold on just a second."

"This baby isn't waiting for you," she growled.

Ryan examined her. "The head has crowned." He moved to the end of the bed and leaned over the footboard. "Phoebe—" his voice was low "—I want you to look at me. On the next contraction I want you to push."

Her gaze met his between her knees. They didn't have to wait long. "Push."

Ryan reached for the baby's head and supported it. His look went to Phoebe again. "You're doing beautifully."

Another contraction hit. His gaze held hers. He wished he could hold her hand and comfort her but he couldn't be at two places at once. "Push, honey."

Ryan glanced down. The baby's shoulders slid out and the rest of the tiny human followed. He saw birth all the time but none had been more amazing.

Exhausted, Phoebe fall back on the bed.

"It's a boy," Ryan announced. He tied off the umbilical cord before cutting it and laid the baby on Phoebe's stomach.

She reached a hand up to touch the tiny head.

At the baby's squeaking sound, Ryan came around to the bedside table and reached for the suction bubble. He cleaned the air passages and mouth. Grabbing a clean towel, he wiped the newborn.

The sight before him was more beautiful than any he'd ever witnessed. His heart swelled. For once he could understand the feeling new parents had when their child was born.

"He's perfect, Phoebe." Ryan couldn't keep the reverence out of his voice.

She looked at him with a tired smile. "He is, isn't he?"

Ryan leaned down and kissed her on the forehead. "No more perfect than you. I'm going to lay him beside you and go get a washcloth and finish washing him up. You and I still have some work to do." He took a towel from the end of the bed. Wrapping the baby in it, he placed him beside her.

Phoebe secured him with her arm.

"Don't move." Quickly he went to the bathroom and prepared a warm washcloth. Returning to Phoebe, he cleaned the baby boy, swaddled him in a sheet and placed him in the cradle.

Going to the end of the bed, Ryan said, "Okay, Phoebe, I need a couple of big pushes and we'll be done here. Then you can rest."

Half an hour later Ryan had Phoebe settled with the baby at her breast. He stood at the end of the bed and watched them. He was so full of emotion all he could do was stare. It had been an honor to be a part of such a special event. Phoebe's eyelids lifted.

They were full of love that extended to him.

"What's your middle name?"

"James."

Phoebe looked down at the baby. "Joshua James Taylor." She looked back at Ryan. "We'll call him JJ."

Ryan's eyes watered.

"Why don't you join us and get to know your namesake?"

Ryan didn't hesitate to join them on the bed. Phoebe lifted her head and he slipped an arm under her neck. JJ mewed as if he wished the two adults would stop interrupting his sleep. He soon quieted. Ryan ran his palm over JJ's silky head. Despite having delivered hundreds of babies, Ryan had never spent any time enjoying the touch and feel of a newborn. He picked up the tiny hand and JJ wrapped it around Ryan's finger. His heart was captured.

Ryan had spent so much of his life alone and now he wanted more. He would never go back to living closed off from people. His world was right here in his arms and he was going to hold on to it tight.

He looked at Phoebe. Her eyes were clear and confident. "We are yours. All you have to do is accept us."

"I love you, Phoebe. And I love JJ. I want to be a part of your lives if you will let me."

"And we love you. We are family now."

Ryan kissed her tenderly on the lips. When he lifted his mouth from hers Phoebe's eyelids had already closed. He shut his, releasing a sigh of contentment. He'd gone from being a man alone and caring nothing about the future to a man who had everything he could hope for, including a bright future. Life was worth living.

* * * * *

Don't miss the next story in the fabulous
MIDWIVES ON-CALL *series*
UNLOCKING HER SURGEON'S HEART
by Fiona Lowe
Available in January 2016!

MILLS & BOON®
Large Print Medical

January

Unlocking Her Surgeon's Heart	Fiona Lowe
Her Playboy's Secret	Tina Beckett
The Doctor She Left Behind	Scarlet Wilson
Taming Her Navy Doc	Amy Ruttan
A Promise...to a Proposal?	Kate Hardy
Her Family for Keeps	Molly Evans

February

Hot Doc from Her Past	Tina Beckett
Surgeons, Rivals...Lovers	Amalie Berlin
Best Friend to Perfect Bride	Jennifer Taylor
Resisting Her Rebel Doc	Joanna Neil
A Baby to Bind Them	Susanne Hampton
Doctor...to Duchess?	Annie O'Neil

March

Falling at the Surgeon's Feet	Lucy Ryder
One Night in New York	Amy Ruttan
Daredevil, Doctor...Husband?	Alison Roberts
The Doctor She'd Never Forget	Annie Claydon
Reunited...in Paris!	Sue MacKay
French Fling to Forever	Karin Baine

MILLS & BOON®
Large Print Medical

April

The Baby of Their Dreams	Carol Marinelli
Falling for Her Reluctant Sheikh	Amalie Berlin
Hot-Shot Doc, Secret Dad	Lynne Marshall
Father for Her Newborn Baby	Lynne Marshall
His Little Christmas Miracle	Emily Forbes
Safe in the Surgeon's Arms	Molly Evans

May

A Touch of Christmas Magic	Scarlet Wilson
Her Christmas Baby Bump	Robin Gianna
Winter Wedding in Vegas	Janice Lynn
One Night Before Christmas	Susan Carlisle
A December to Remember	Sue MacKay
A Father This Christmas?	Louisa Heaton

June

Playboy Doc's Mistletoe Kiss	Tina Beckett
Her Doctor's Christmas Proposal	Louisa George
From Christmas to Forever?	Marion Lennox
A Mummy to Make Christmas	Susanne Hampton
Miracle Under the Mistletoe	Jennifer Taylor
His Christmas Bride-to-Be	Abigail Gordon